Coffee Is Served

Coffee Is Served

BY

TRACY WILSON

http://beautifulpublications.com

Published by
Beautiful Publications LLC
Stratford, CT 06614

This book is a work of fiction. Names, characters, places, and incidents are either products of the author's imagination or are used fictitiously. Any resemblance to actual events or locales or persons, living or dead, is entirely coincidental.

LIBRARY OF CONGRESS CONTROL NUMBER:
2021915274

PRINT ISBN: 978-1-7373828-4-3
EBOOK ISBN: 978-1-7373828-5-0

Printed in the United States of America

Dedication

This book is dedicated to coffee lovers.

Contents

WARNING: EXPLICIT CONTENT

I did a 'coffee' search in my books and I began to realize that my characters drink more coffee than anything else, so I'm giving you a book filled with coffee; however, I must warn you – you'll never look at coffee the same way again! You'll be reading chapters from the following books:

Bazil & Lydia Osgood – Erotic Zombies 3
Caught In The Middle
Helen
Harmony
How Far Are You Willing To Go? 3
How Far Are You Willing To Go? 5
My Christmas Miracle
Obsidian Heart
Obsidian Heart 2
The Ultimate Con
The Ultimate Con 2
Thirst Quencher
Thirst Quencher 2
Twisted Beautiee
Twisted Beautiee 3
Twisted Beautiee 5
Twister Starr
Twisted Starr 2
Twisted Mary
Twisted Mary 3

Introduction

I fell in love with the cover as soon as I saw it. The love between the couple reminds me of how we were when we first got together.

I grew up around coffee. My grandparents had coffee every day. When we were little, you had to buy the coffee filters, add water to the pot, and wait for it to perk.

My grandfather made his own coffee mugs and he whistled as he poured himself coffee throughout the day. I'd ask him if I could use one of his mugs and he'd allow me to as long as I understood I better be careful and not break his mug!

My mother made coffee with Mr. Coffee until I became a teenager. My sister and I started helping ourselves to coffee whenever she made a pot and when we didn't have any creamer, milk, or sugar, we'd drink it black. As I got older, we moved away from Mr. Coffee and started drinking Maxwell House instant coffee or whatever was on sale when they ran out of Maxwell House.

When my sisters and I had children, my mother would give her grandchildren coffee and it made them feel special, so I carried on the tradition with my grandchildren.

Bazil & Lydia Osgood Erotic Zombies 3

"Good morning Mrs. Osgood..." Bazil breathed as he kissed Beautiee awake...

"Good morning..." she breathed as she stretched and arched her back...

"Mmmm... that gives me an idea..." he said as he got on top of her and slid down between her legs...

"Bazil... don't..." Bazil stopped and came back up between her legs...

"Ohh... you want some more dick..." he breathed as he kissed her...

"Bazil... get up..."

"What's wrong?"

"I gotta go!" she answered as she jumped up, ran into the bathroom, and hurled last night's dinner into the toilet...

"Beautiee? Are you okay?" he asked as he came running into the bathroom...

"I think so..."

"You sure?"

1

"Bazil..."

"Yes Beautiee?"

"Open that drawer..."

"Okay – you have vagisil, toothpaste, Tylenol and... a pregnancy test?"

"Yes Bazil..."

"Beautiee – when did you..."

"Remember we order two pregnancy tests before we went on our second honeymoon?"

"Oh my God..."

"Open it..." she smiled as Bazil tore into the box like a kid at Christmas....

"Here!"

"Thanks..." she laughed...

"You need me to leave?"

"No – stay..."

"Okay – can I watch?"

"Yes Bazil..." she laughed... "You can watch..." she laughed again as she sat down on the toilet, spread her legs, and peed...

"Oh my God – give it to me!" he squealed...

"Wait a minute!" she laughed as she got up and placed the pregnancy test on the sink. Bazil and Beautiee stood there holding each other tight as they both bent down to look at the results...

"Beautiee..." Bazil whispered as he started crying...

"We're gonna have another baby..." Beautiee said as she started crying too...

"I love you..."

"I love you too..." she said as they started kissing profusely...

"Let's take a shower..."

"Okay..." Bazil turned on the water, stepped inside, and extended his hand for her to take, and she stepped into the shower...

"Hello Baby..." Bazil said as he started rubbing her stomach...

"Lydia..."

"Lydia?"

"Yes..."

"Hi Lydia..." Bazil said as he pushed her back against the shower stall and kissed his way down...

"Bazil?" Beautiee yawned... "Bazil? Where are you? Hmmm – maybe he's downstairs making coffee..." she said out loud as she got out of bed, put on her robe and slippers, and went downstairs... "Okay – I guess you're not making coffee..." she sighed when she went into the kitchen, took two cups out the cabinet, and started making coffee... "What the hell is he doing out there?" she asked out loud as she went over to the French doors and looked outside. Bazil had the bottle of Weed Killer in one hand and was spraying all around the pool area with the other. When he got to the area in front of the shed he stopped for a few moments, and then he sprayed the area where we came up through the dirt. After he was done, he went back in the shed, came out with the spade, and began chopping at Clayton's body... "Bazil?"

"Beautiee – go back inside..." She didn't listen to him – instead she went outside and walked past him... "Beautiee – what are you doing?"

"I'm making coffee..." she answered as she went in the shed, took a lawn bag down from the shelf, and came back outside...

"I thought you said you were making coffee?"

3

"I am..." she answered as she dropped the lawn bag on Clayton's body. Beautiee went back into the kitchen and finished making the coffee as Bazil put Clayton's body in the lawn bag, tied it, and put it in the garbage bin...

"Mmmm... smells good..." he said as he came inside...

"It is..." she said as she handed him a cup of coffee and they went to sit down at the table... "What'd you do with the body?"

"I put it in the garbage..."

"Did you put the garbage out?"

"Not yet..."

"I can't believe it's over..."

"Neither can I..."

"I can't believe we're having another baby..."

"I love you..."

"I love you too..."

"What would you like to do first?"

"I'd like to go to News 12..."

"Really?"

"Yea..."

"You're happy..."

"Yea..."

"So am I..."

"After we go to News 12, I want to go tell our kids they can come home... and then I want to bring them home..."

"Okay..."

"I want to sound-proof our room..."

"Okay..."

"I want to re-decorate Joy's room..."

"Okay..."

"I want to have my cover designer design a cover for the book about your parents..."

"Okay..." Bazil laughed...

"And I want to finish what I started in the living room the other night..." Bazil got up from the table, went over to her, and pulled her into a kiss... "Mmmm..."

"I'm going to ask you again..." he breathed in her ear... "What..." he said as he kissed her mouth... "Do..." he said as he kissed her left nipple... "You" he said as he kissed her right nipple... "Want..." he said as he kissed her stomach... "To..." he said as he spread her lips... "Do..." he said as he flicked her clit with his tongue... "First..." he said as he pulled her body towards him and started sucking...

"Bazil... Huh... Huh... Huh..."

"Mmmm..." he moaned as he stuck his tongue inside her and slurped...

"Bazil... I'm cumming..." she moaned as he started sucking again... "Haa... Haa... Haa... Haa... Haaaaahhhh!"

"Uh uh..." Bazil said as he held her up by her ass to keep her from slumping down...

"Bazil..." she moaned as he continued licking and sucking softly...

"Answer me..." he breathed...

"You!" she moaned...

"Are you sure?"

"Yeesss...."

"Okay then..." he said as he stood up, kissed her, and put his tongue in her mouth...

"Mmmm..." she moaned...

"Come with me..." he said as he took her by the hand and led her into the living room. Bazil removed his slippers, took off his robe, dropped it on the floor, took off his pajamas, and stood in front of her naked. Beautiee walked over to him, pushed him down onto the couch, put the pillows on the floor, kneeled on the pillows, and took him in her mouth slowly...

"Got Damn..." he breathed as she took him all the way in her mouth and swirled her tongue around his shaft before she took him all the way out... "Yes Beautiee... Suck it..." he moaned as he put his hands in her hair and pushed her head back down on his dick... "Fuck... Beautiee..."

"Mmmm... Hmmm..." she moaned on his dick, pushing him over the edge...

"Uuuuggghhhh!" Beautiee continued sucking softly for a few moments until he called her name again... "Beautiee..."

"Yesss... Bazil..." she answered as she looked up at him...

"Come here..." he breathed as he pulled her up into a kiss... "What would you like to do next?"

"I want to go to News 12 and let them know this is over..."

"Really?"

"Yea..."

"Okay..."

"I still can't believe it..."

"Neither can I..."

"If anybody told me what I was in for when I married you..." Beautiee laughed...

"What's that supposed to mean?"

"I never expected to see your dead parents fuckin' in our backyard – let alone meet them..." she laughed... "It's a true romance with a happy ending..." she sighed...

"A true romance? A happy ending? I think you've had a little more than coffee..." Bazil laughed...

"Your parents came to ask for your help because they couldn't rest..."

"True..."

"All they wanted was to spend eternity together... but Clayton stood in their way..."

"True..."

"Don't you see? We saved their lives – in death – Oh my God!" she squealed as she jumped up, ran into the library and turned on her computer...

"Beautiee – what are you doing?"

"I need to write these ideas before I forget them – and I need you to send me pictures of your parents on their wedding day so I can get them over to my cover designer – you know what – never mind – I'll just scan these pictures to my computer and send them over..." she said as she stood up and Bazil pulled her into a kiss...

"Mmmm... what was that for?" she breathed...

"I love you so much..."

"I love you to – but I need to do this..." she said as she went over to the wall and took down the pictures of his parents...

"Please Beautiee – be careful with those..."

"I will..." she said as she took her time taking them out the frame. Bazil watched as she scanned them to her computer and waited for her to finish... "Here..." she said as she handed him back the pictures and he put them in the frame and hung them back up... "When were your parents married?" she asked as she started typing...

"Sunday, March 23, 1930..."

"Okay – thanks..."

"Beautiee..."

"Yes Bazil..." she answered without stopping...

"We need to get ready...

"You get started – I'll join you in a few minutes..."

"You promise?"

"Yes – I promise – I need to get back to this!" she exclaimed...

"Okay, okay!" Bazil laughed as he headed upstairs...

"You ready for this?" Beautiee asked as they started walking across the parking lot at the train station in Norwalk...

"I'm ready if you are..."

"Okay – let's do this..." she said as she took his hand, they crossed the street, and ran right into Della Crews from News 12 Connecticut...

"Bazil! How are you?"

"I'm fine..."

"What brings you here?"

"Hello Della..." Beautiee said deliberately...

"Hello Mrs. Osgood – how are you?"

"I'm fine..." she sighed as Bazil pulled her close to him and put his arm around her...

"I was just going to have lunch – care to join me?"

"Another time..." Bazil said...

"I'm going to hold you to that..."

"Let us know when..." Beautiee said as she walked off...

"Let's go inside..." Bazil said as he took Beautiee by the hand, they walked up Cross Street, and went inside...

"Mr. Osgood – Mrs. Osgood – I thought you forgot about me..." Gwen laughed...

"We ran into Della..." Bazil laughed...

"Really? She told me she was going to lunch..."

"She invited us to join her..." Beautiee laughed...

"That woman will stop at nothing..." Gwen laughed, shaking her head...

"Let's go into your office before she gets back..." Bazil said...

"You're right – come with me..." she said as we followed her into her office...

"Hi Marissa – where's Gwen?" Della asked...

8

"I thought you were going to lunch?"

"I was..." she sighed...

"What happened?"

"They pissed me off – now I have an attitude – I'm hungry – and that's a bad combination!"

"I work with you – I know..." Marissa laughed...

"I'm sorry..."

"I have something that might make you feel better..."

"Do tell?" Della said as she slid over in the chair towards Marissa...

"The Osgood's are here..." she whispered...

"I knew it!" she snapped...

"I'm Gwen Edwards, News 12 Connecticut, bringing you an exclusive. I'm sitting here with Mr. & Mrs. Osgood – thank you both for coming in today..."

"Thank you for having us..."

"Mr. & Mrs. Osgood – it's always a pleasure – but I know our viewers are as curious as I am – what brings you here today?"

"As you know, we own Osgood Publishing..." Bazil answered...

"Yes – I'm aware..."

"After residents started reporting zombies in their backyard, we went to our office and checked the area surrounding our building..."

"Oh no – I hope everything was alright..."

"Unfortunately –it wasn't – we could see that zombies had been on the property..."

"What did you do?"

"The first thing we did was reduce the work hours for our staff. After we did that, we spoke with our landscapers and had them re-plant the flowers and bushes..."

"You weren't afraid they'd come back?"

"No..."

"Have you seen anything since?"

"Yesterday, we went to take a look and my landscapers told me everything was good..."

"How can you be sure they won't be back?"

"Because the supervisor told me he sprayed the area with Weed Killer sold by the Landscaping Corporation..."

"Mr. Osgood – are you telling me Weed Killer keeps the zombies from re-appearing?"

"According to our landscapers... yes..."

"Oh my God – is the Landscaping Corporation aware of this?"

"They will be after you air this interview..." Bazil laughed...

"Oh wow – okay – I'll get right on that..."

"There's something else we need to tell you..." Beautiee said...

"Yes Mrs. Osgood – go ahead..."

"Last night – we were in our backyard in the shed and..." Bazil took Beautiee's hand and squeezed it...

"Are you okay to continue?" Gwen asked as she touched her shoulder...

"Yes..." she breathed...

"Go ahead..."

"We came face to face with a zombie..."

"Oh my God! What did you do?"

"The only thing I could think of was to grab the Weed Killer and spray..."

"Did it kill the zombie?"

"It didn't kill the zombie – it burned it..."

"It burned it?"

"It started screaming and rubbing its eyes... and..."

"I picked up the spade and cracked its scull..." Bazil interrupted..."

"Wait – the two of you actually killed a zombie?"

"Yes..." Bazil answered...

"Thank God I remembered what the supervisor told us about the Weed Killer..." Beautiee said...

"Thank God is right – I'm Gwen Edwards, News 12 Connecticut. As you just heard, Weed Killer, sold by the Landscaping Corporation, burns zombies and stops them from coming back when sprayed on lawns. News 12 Connecticut will continue to bring you updates..."

"Charles! Charles! Get in here!"

"I saw it..." Charles sighed...

"Isn't that great?" Theresa exclaimed...

"Yes - it is – I accused him of lying to our son and he actually did what he said he was going to do – that's just fucking great!"

Caught In The Middle

"Lacey..." Dexter whispered...

"Huh?" I answered sleepily..."

"I'm gonna go – I'll see you later..." he whispered again and then he bent down to kiss me...

"Okay..." I sighed as I watched him slip out...

"Honey..." I whispered as I touched Darien on the shoulder...

"Uuuggghhh..." he groaned as he stretched... "What time is it?"

"It's a little after 7..."

"That's gives me an idea..." he breathed as he pushed me down on my back and kissed me...

"Mmmm... don't you have to get ready for work?"

"You're not trying to get rid of me – are you?"

"Never..." I breathed as I pulled him into a kiss...

"So you still want me?"

"Oh Darien – Baby I'm sorry..."

"Do you love him?" I didn't want to answer him... "Look at me..." he said as he turned my face to him and looked me in my eyes...

"Yes..." I answered as I teared up...

"Thank you..." he breathed as he kissed me...

"For what?"

"For being honest with me..." he answered as he got up out of bed...

"Where are you going?"

"I'm going to get in the shower – care to join me?"

"Okay..." I smiled as I jumped up out of bed and followed him into the bathroom. Darien turned on the shower, waited for the water to get hot, got in, and started washing himself. I got in and stood in front of him underneath the shower head as the water ran down on my head. Darien turned me around, spread my legs, spread my cheeks, and began fucking me in my ass... "Darien..." I moaned...

"Uggh! Uggh! Uggh! Uggh!" Darien held me around my waist and kissed the back of my neck as he slowed down, but didn't stop...

"Darien..." I moaned again...

"Lacey..." he breathed in my ear as he started fucking me harder... "Fuck... I'm cumming... UUUGGGHHH!" I stood there with my legs spread apart as Darien continued holding me and kissing me on my neck... "I've wanted this for so long..." he breathed in my ear...

"I know..."

"Turn around..." he breathed. I turned around, stood still, and waited. Darien took the shampoo, opened it, squeezed some in his hands, put the shampoo back in the holder, and began massaging my scalp and hair...

"Oh Darien... that feels good..." I breathed. Darien rinsed my hair, opened the conditioner, squeezed some in his hands, put the conditioner back in the holder, and began massaging my scalp again... "Ooohhh..." Darien pulled me close to him, kissed me hard, and put his tongue in my mouth as he ran his hands up and down my back... "Mmmm..." Darien took the body wash with one hand, opened it, and squeezed it on me with one hand while holding me with the other. He put the body wash back in the holder and began rubbing it all over me... "Ooohhh..." Darien continued rubbing me all over, paying special attention to my breasts... "Oh Darien..." I moaned as he took my left breast in his mouth while squeezing the right one...

"Spread your legs..." he breathed and then he took my right breast in his mouth and began playing with my pussy...

"Darien... yes..." I moaned as he pushed his fingers inside me...

"Don't you dare cum..." he growled in my ear as he continued finger-fucking me...

"Darien... I'm gonna cum..." I moaned. Darien stopped suddenly and pulled out his fingers. I watched Darien take the bottle of body wash and squeeze some on his dick... "Let me..." I breathed as I began stroking his dick...

"Lacey..." he breathed as he closed his eyes and bent his head back...

"Don't you dare cum..." I laughed as I laid my head on his chest and continued stroking his dick...

"That's it!" he growled as he pushed me back against the shower, spread my legs, and thrust himself inside me...

"DARIEN!" I screamed...

"Yes Lacey – say my name!" he growled as he fucked me hard...

"Haah... Haah... Haah... Haah..."

"That's it Lacey... cum all over me..."

"I'M CUMMING... I'M CUMMING... I'M CUMMING... I'M CCUUMMIINNGG!"

"Say my name..." he breathed...

"Darien... Darien... Darien..."

"FFFUUUCCCKKK!"

"I love you..."

"I love you too..." he breathed as he pulled me into a kiss and kissed me hard... "I'm going to make coffee – I'll see you when you get out..." he said and then he grabbed a towel and hurried out the bathroom. I stepped out the shower, grabbed a towel, wrapped my hair, grabbed another towel, wrapped it around me, and walked into the kitchen... "Here..." Darien said as he placed the cup on the table and I sat down...

"Thank you..." I said as I sat down, picked up the coffee, and sipped...

"We need to talk..." he said as he began making omelets...

"I know..." I sighed...

"Why'd you do it?"

"I'm sorry..." I whispered as I started crying. Darien put down the bowl he was scrambling the eggs in, put down the fork, and came over to me...

"Stand up..." I did as I was told... "Come here..." he said as he pulled me into a hug...

"I'm sorry..." I cried...

"Lacey – listen to me..." he breathed as he kissed me...

"Okay..."

"I know you're sorry – and I forgive you..."

15

"Oh Darien – I love you so much..."

"I love you too – but I need you to listen..."

"Okay..."

"We need to talk..."

"I know... but..."

"Uh uh – stop doing that..."

"Okay..."

"We need to talk about this so we can get past it..."

"Okay..."

"That means when I ask you a question – I need you to answer me – and I need you to be honest with me..."

"Okay..."

"Now I want you to sit down, drink your coffee, and answer my question while I finish making breakfast..."

"Okay..." I sighed as I sat down and Darien went back to making the omelets... "I was at the gym and he came in..."

"Go on..." he said as he got the cheese out the refrigerator, put it in a bowl, and started grating it...

"He'd work out and we'd make jokes about him..."

"What kind of jokes?"

"Ummm... sex..."

"Was he the only man in the gym?" he asked as he put the cheese in the eggs, scrambled it together, and then poured it in the pan...

"No..." I sighed...

"He came to the gym – dressed to work out – and he made sure you could see all his assets..."

"Yea..."

"And ‑ he ease-dropped on your conversations – and of all the women in the gym – he approached you..."

"Well... kinda..."

"He'd talk with the other women here and there – but he set his sights on you..." he said as he put two plates on the table, sat down, and gave me a fork...

"Thank you..." I breathed as I cut into the omelet and tasted it...

"How is it?"

"It's delicious..."

"Good..."

"What makes you think he set his sights on me?"

"Because..." he answered before tasting his omelet... "I was that guy..."

"I don't understand..."

"It seemed completely innocent at first – but one day – you were coming out of the shower – you had a towel on – you thought everyone was gone – you dropped your towel – you started getting dressed – he came in with nothing on but a towel..."

"Oh my God..." I whispered...

"He told you he thought everyone was gone – he was so sorry – he didn't mean to make you uncomfortable – he reached out to touch you on your shoulder – his towel fell off – and before you had a chance to react he had his hands all over you – right?"

"Yes..." I whispered...

"You didn't object so he picked you up, ripped off your panties, wrapped your legs around his waist – and fucked you – so tell me – was it in the shower or on the bench?"

"On the bench..." I sighed as I covered my face with my hands. Darien put down his fork and took my hands away from my face...

"Look at me..."

"No... I can't..."

"Look at me Lacey..."

"How could I have been so stupid?" I asked with tears in my eyes...

"Stop crying..." he said as he wiped my tears... "I need you to listen to me..."

"Okay..."

"I was that guy..."

"You were?"

"Yes..."

"Why?"

"Before I met you – that's what I did..."

"You went to the gym to meet women?"

"I went to the gym to prey on married women..."

"Are you saying Dexter set me up because I'm married?"

"Yes..."

"Why? Out of all the women that go to the gym – why me?"

"Because we don't go to the gym looking for a relationship..."

"I'm confused..."

"A single woman is going to become attached – she's going to expect a commitment – she'll expect you to be exclusive – that's not what we want – that's not what I wanted..."

"What did you want?"

"I wanted pussy – nothing more – nothing less – that's why I went for married women..."

"Oh my God – how could you do that?"

"I wasn't the one that took those vows – I didn't give a fuck about her husband – as long as I got what I wanted and she was willing – I'd give her all the dick she could stand until she ended it – and then I'd move on to the next..."

"Oh my God – Darien – I'm sorry – I didn't mean to..."

"Yes you did..." he interrupted...

"I swear – I didn't..."

"Stop talking before you make me hurt you..." he said as he put his finger to my mouth... "You were excited – you got caught up in the moment – you fucked him – and you liked it – isn't that right?" I shook my head yes to acknowledge he was right as I started crying again... "I told you – I was that guy – I had many women – I was in their houses too – their husbands were completely clueless – their wives were sexually deprived and they were mine for the taking – so I took them every time they offered themselves to me – but what happened yesterday – with you – well..."

"Why?"

"As I told you – I was watching you for about 15 minutes..."

"Darien – please – let me..."

"I'm not done talking..."

"Okay..."

"My first thought was to blow his fuckin' head off in front of you – but since I've been that guy myself – I decided to join you..."

"I was afraid..."

"I know you were – but it wasn't about you – it was about him – and he fell for it – actually – he fell for you – and I can't have that..."

"I don't understand..."

"I was that man – and I never fell for a married woman – and even if I had – I would've never agreed to what happened yesterday..."

"You had a gun... you wouldn't let him leave..."

"Lacey – I'm a man – and as a man – I'm going out fighting – and he didn't even try to put up a fight!" he laughed...

"He didn't want to get shot..."

"Lacey – stop – I can't..." he laughed...

"Stop laughing at me!" I snapped...

"Lacey – I love you..." he said as he kissed me... "I forgive you – but right now – I don't give a fuck about your feelings – I need you to understand what I'm telling you..."

"Damn – that's fucked up..."

"Lacey – I need you to understand – I know I hurt your feelings – but you broke my heart..."

"I'm sorry..." I said as I started crying again...

"Lacey – he didn't put up a fight because he loves you..."

"What?"

"I watched him kiss you – I watched him taste you – I watched him make love to you – he made two fatal mistakes..."

"Two?"

"First – he fell for the mark..."

"So I was nothing more than a mark..." I sighed...

"Did you really think it was more than that?"

"Yes..." I sighed...

"Wow – I'm disappointed – but he made you fall in love with him so he still has some skills..."

"Oh my God – you make me sound like a whore..."

"I never called you a whore Lacey..."

"So he thinks I'm a whore?"

"Lacey – I need you to focus!"

"Okay..."

"If I ever got caught by the husband – I would never, ever, ever agree to a threesome with them..."

"What would you have done?"

"I would've gone out like a man..."

"So you would've risked being shot?"

"Hell yea – but Dexter thinks I'm cool with you being with him – and he loves you – and that's a problem..."

"I'll never see him again..."

"That's not good enough..."

"Please –tell me what you want – I'll do anything..."

"You'll do nothing..." he breathed as he kissed me...

"I don't understand..."

"When he contacts you – you tell him it's over..."

"I will – I promise..."

"And then you tell me..."

"Okay..."

"Now – I know this is going to be hard... but I need to ask you something..."

"Okay..."

"Did you suck his dick?"

"No..."

"Are you telling me the truth?"

"Yes..."

"Did you always use a condom?"

"Yes..."

"How many times was he in our bed?"

"Yesterday was the first time..." I answered as I started crying again. Darien came over to me, sat down, and took my face in his hands...

"I know this is hard... but I need to know..."

"I know..."

"What did you need that I didn't give you?"

"Darien... please... it wasn't your fault... it was me..."

"Yes... it was you... but you haven't answered my question..."

"I don't know... I just..."

"I thought you were going to be honest with me..."

"I'm sorry..."

"Lacey – I love you – but you're making me angry..." he said as he began squeezing my face..."

"Darien... please... you're hurting me..."

"I'm sorry – I don't mean to hurt you – but I need you to answer my question..." he said as he wiped my tears with his thumbs...

"I was... lonely..."

"You were lonely?"

"I wanted you..."

"I was right here..."

"You come home... we eat dinner... we cuddle... we go to bed... you turn over... you go to sleep..."

"So you felt like I didn't want you..."

"Yes..."

"Thank you for telling me..." he said as he let go of my face, got up, and left me in the kitchen.

I didn't get much sleep. I decided to get up and make myself some coffee. I turned over to look at the side of the bed where Harland was and even though I was sad, I began to smile. I slept with my phone next to me and kept it charged in case he sent me a message. Maybe I was dickmatized – but I didn't give a damn. It just couldn't end like this before it began. He has to make it up to me – we need to have a real date – a first date – without his mother...

"Bzzz! Bzzz! Bzzz!" I grabbed the phone and saw I had a text message from Harland...

"Harmony..." he started with a sad emoji face... "I'm sorry. I had no idea my mother was coming. I wanted to be with you so bad, it hurt. I was so happy when you took my phone from me and turned it off because that let me know you wanted to be with me too. You are something special and I don't want what happened last night to ruin what we shared before we get a chance to be happy. I'd like to come see you tonight to talk – if you're willing to hear me out. If you'd rather not see me again – fuck it – I can't lie – I need to see you... please..." he ended his text with another sad emoji and praying hands. I was on cloud nine. I held the phone close to my breast and imagine him sucking it...

"See – nope!" I said out loud as I went downstairs. I put the phone down, I went into the kitchen, and I made myself some coffee. After I sat down and started drinking my coffee, I replied to his text...

"Harland..." I started with a smiling emoji... "What happened last night was a lot to deal with. I was expecting to have a first date with you and I was also expecting we'd talk and get to know each other. I've wanted to be with you ever since the night you kissed me (I'm sure you knew that) – that's why I hugged you when I saw you. I didn't sleep well last night so I stayed home today. I'd love to see you so we can talk. What time do you get off work? Let me know and I'll meet you – I know you're at work but we can meet for lunch if that's okay..." I ended my text with a smiling emoji...

"You have made my day! What would you like for lunch?"

"Actually – I'd like some breakfast – I've been craving shrimp & grits and a steak, egg, & cheese sandwich from Queens Delight..."

"I'm on my way!"

"On your way? I thought you were at work?"

"I'm clocking out – I'll see you soon..."

"Okay..."

"What the fuck did I just do?" I sighed... "Oh well – good think I took a shower last night – I hope he doesn't wanna go out 'cause I'm not getting dressed..." I laughed as I finished my coffee. I turned on HGTV and whatever was on was watching me because I was barely paying attention. I was so happy I wanted to call Snow and Yyanna but I didn't because, to be honest, I was afraid they'd talk me out of it. I kicked back in my recliner and fell back to sleep...

I jumped as soon as I heard him knock... "Who is it?"
"Harland..." I jumped up out the recliner, hurried to the door, and snatched it open. Harland picked me up, I wrapped my legs around his waist, I wrapped my arms around his neck, and we tongued each other down as he walked inside and pushed the door closed with his foot. We continued kissing as he walked me over to the couch and sat me down. My legs were still wrapped around him as he got on his knees, opened my robe, took my breasts in his hands, and alternated between sucking the left nipple and the right...
"Harland..." I moaned. His tongue felt so good I arched my back so he would take more of my breast into his mouth. Harland was happy to oblige me and sucked on both of them so hard he left hickies on them before he started kissing his way down my stomach... "Huh... Huh..." I moaned. When he got to my pussy, he ran his tongue from the top of my clit down to the bottom and then he stuck his tongue inside... "Harland..." I moaned... and then

25

he did something I've never had done before... and it startled me. Harland turned his head, took the left side of my labia into his mouth, and sucked it while sliding his tongue up and down... "Ooohhh..." I moaned...

"You like that?"

"Yeesss..." Harland turned his head to the right, took the right side of my labia in his mouth, and sucked it while sliding his tongue up and down... and then he took my clit in his mouth and sucked it... "Ooohhh... Yess... Harland..." I moaned. Harland stopped sucking, spread my lips, and flicked his tongue directly on my clit...

"OOOHHH... OOOHHH... OOOHHH... YEESS... FUCK!" Harland swirled his tongue around my clit and each time he swirled his tongue around, he applied more pressure... "HARLAND... DON'T STOP... DON'T STOP... I'M CUMMING!" I screamed as I grabbed his head and fucked his face. Harland continued swirling his tongue around my clit while applying pressure, giving me mini-gasms as I continued to ride his face. After I released my grip on his head, Harland stuck his tongue in my pussy and I laughed when he started slurping. Harland looked up at me and when he went to enter me, I stopped him...

"What's wrong?"

"Bring it to my mouth..." I breathed as I laid my head back and opened my mouth. Harland kicked his shoes off, stood up on the couch, lowered his dick to my mouth, and I took it in...

"Ohhh shiiittt!!!" he moaned as I swirled my tongue around the head and sucked simultaneously. Harland let me control the pace as I took more of his dick in my mouth... "Yes... Suck it... Yeessss..." I grabbed the bottom of his shaft and began sucking sloppily on his dick while simultaneously swirling my tongue on it... "Harmony... Shit... Suck it..." I let go of his dick, palmed his ass with my hands, and pushed him all the way in... "FFUUUCCCKKK!" he moaned. He began fucking my mouth slowly at first, allowing me to get used to the length and girth. When I pushed him in deeper, he knew what I wanted... "Take this dick!" he growled as he began fucking my mouth harder. I relaxed my throat and did as he commanded. I felt the vein on the side of his dick rising and I knew he was close to cumming... "Fuck... Shit... I'm cummin'... I'm cummin'... Uuuggghhh!" I held him in my mouth as he convulsed, swallowed his cum, and kept on sucking... "Harmony..." I looked up at him as he played in my hair and I continued sucking him softly. I began sucking a little more when I felt him getting hard again and he stopped me... "Let me fuck you... please..." he breathed. I looked up at him and eased my mouth off his dick until I got to the head. I wrapped my hand around his dick and held it as I flicked my tongue on the head of it... and Harland lost it... "I said I wanna fuck you!" he growled as he snatched his dick away from my mouth, held my legs up, and thrust himself inside me...

"Harland... Harland... Harland..." I moaned...

"Uugh... Uugh... Uugh..."

"Fuck me Harland... Just like that... Yesss..."

"Uugh... Uugh... Uugh..."

"Harder... Yes... Fuck... I'm cumming..."

"Uugh... Uugh... Uugh..."

"HARLAND!" I screamed as I came...

"UUUGH! UUUGH! UUUGH! UUUGH! UUUGH!" Harland stayed inside me and pushed his tongue in my mouth...

"Hmmph... Hmmph... Hmmph..." I moaned as he fucked out his orgasm. We began sucking each other's tongues and after a few moments I spoke... "Harland..."

"Yes Baby..."

"Where's the food?"

"Oh shit – I left it in the car!" he laughed as he got up. When he stood up, I inched over to the edge of the couch and took his dick in my mouth before he could *zip* his pants... "Now see – you startin' trouble again..." he breathed as he grabbed my head and pushed his dick in my mouth. I braced myself on the edge of the couch and let him fuck my mouth as much as he wanted to... and then he stopped suddenly...

"Why'd you stop?"

"I need to get the food..." he said as he turned away from me and went to get the food. I laughed when I saw him zip his pants before he went out the door. When he came back inside with the food, he locked the door and went into the dining room. I got up and followed him... "I hope it's still hot..." he said as he took the food out the bags and put it on the table...

"It is..." I said as I picked up the tins and felt underneath them...

"Good – 'cause I promised you breakfast..." he said as he went to sit down and I put my hand out to stop him... "I can't sit down?"

"Nope... I answered as I pulled him towards me and unzipped his pants. Harland looked down at me and smiled as I took his dick out and looked up at him... "Now... where were we?" I asked as I put his dick in my mouth. Harland didn't need to be told what to do – he grabbed my head and fucked my mouth...

"Mmm... Mmm... Mmm..." I moaned on his dick as I slurped...

"Fuck! Suck my dick!" I relaxed my jaws and took him all the way in as my spit ran down his balls... "I'm cummin'... I'm cummin'... I'm cummin'... Ffffuuucckkk!" Harland held my head as I swallowed and continued sucking softly until I pulled my mouth away... "Come here..." he commanded as he pulled me up from the chair and kissed me hard...

"Let's talk..." I breathed...

"Okay..." We sat down, opened the tins, opened the aluminum foil, and started eating. We didn't talk at all until we finished everything...

"Damn that was slamming – thank you!"

"Thank you..."

"For?"

"For wanting me..." he breathed as he leaned in and kissed me again...

"Let's talk..."

"Okay..." he sighed... "My mother is manic-depressive. When she takes her medication – she's okay – when she doesn't – she behaves like she did last night..."

"Harland – I'm sorry – I had no idea..."

"I know you didn't – but that's no excuse – my mother knew exactly what she was doing..."

"How do you deal with that?"

"As long as it's just me and her – she's fine – but now that you've come into my life – she feels threatened – when she feels threatened – she lashes out..."

"So she wants you all to herself?"

"Pretty much..."

"Well she needs to move over – 'cause I want you..."

"Harmony..." he whispered as he teared up...

"Don't cry..." I said as I leaned over to hug him...

"I'm so happy right now – it's been so long..."

"It's been a long time for me too..."

"I told my mother she needs to get her own place..."

"Harland no – don't put your mother out because of me..."

"I love you for saying that – but I didn't put her out because of you – well you were part of the reason – I put her out for me..."

"Are you sure?"

"Last night was the straw that broke the camel's back – she needs to go..."

"I'm sorry..."

"You don't need to apologize – I should've put my mother in her place a long time ago – plus – I'm a man – I don't need to be living with my mother anyway..."

"Why are you living with your mother?"

"I wasn't – at first – I have a 2-bedroom downtown – but my father left my mother because she's too controlling..."

"He didn't know she was manic-depressive?"

"He didn't give a damn – my mother plays on that – she can be very manipulative and controlling..."

"I'm so sorry..."

"When he left, he turned the house over to me but I gave it to her..."

"You're so sweet..."

"I gave it to her – but everything's still in my name – I pay the bills in both places..."

"You are really good to your mother..."

"I love my mother – I know you wanted to hurt her last night – and you had every right – but I couldn't let you..."

"Harland – all I was going to do was push her out of the house..."

"And she would've swung on you – and you would've been fighting..."

"Oh hell yea – you right..."

"I'll still take care of my mother – but after last night – she has to go..."

"I wish it didn't have to come to that..."

"Don't feel bad – I don't..."

"You don't? Why?"

"She slapped me so hard she made my mouth bleed..."

"Oh my God! Why?"

"Because I told her she needed to go ride a dick..."

"Harland!"

"Well she does!" Harland laughed...

"How did she know where I lived?"

"I had a GPS tracker put in our phone after my father left – I need to be able to get to her if there's an emergency..."

"Oh so when you didn't answer your phone, she turned on the GPS tracker..."

"Yea..."

"So what happens now?"

"You take me upstairs..." he answered as he got up and then he pulled me up into his arms... "You let me make love to you..." he breathed as he kissed me... "You let me fuck you..." he breathed as he kissed me again... "We get in the shower..." he breathed as he kissed me again... "We fuck in the shower..." he breathed a she kissed me again... "We get out the shower..." he breathed as he kissed me again... "We go back to bed..." he breathed as he kissed me again... "And we do it again..." he breathed as he kissed me again... "And again..." he breathed as he kissed me again... "And again..."

"Okay!" I squealed as I took him by the hand and pulled him out the dining room...

Harmony

"I can't let this go – I need to talk to him – I need him to forgive me..." I was frantic. I'd barely gotten any sleep. I was rushing around the house, my pressure was high, and I was shaking... "Le'me smoke this blunt..." I said out loud as I lit it and pulled on it hard... "Fuck it – I'll go see my girl – she'll give me a note for my job – it's not like I don't have anxiety..." I said as I finished the blunt...

"Where the hell is this uber?" I exclaimed. I'd only been waiting for a minute or so – but it felt like an hour... "Bout damn time!" I exclaimed as I got in...

"Court House Harmony?"

"Yes..."

"Okay – we'll be there in 10 minutes..." he said as he drove off quick. Normally I'd be pissed with reckless driving but I was in a hurry to get to Harland so I didn't complain... "We're here..."

"Thanks – have a good day!" I exclaimed as I jumped out the uber. I started to go up the steps but then I saw

Harland going into the hotel... "Harland!" I called out... "Shit – he didn't hear me!" I exclaimed as I hurried across the street and went inside the hotel... "Harland!" I exclaimed as I ran up to him and threw my arms around him...

"Excuse me – I'm..."

"Harland – please – just let me talk to you – I know it's my fault your mother's dead – I'm sorry – I didn't mean it – I never wanted her to die – I just wanted to make her stop – I..."

"Stop talking..." he commanded. I stopped talking and he took my hand... "Have you had breakfast?"

"The only thing I've had is a blunt..." I laughed nervously...

"Come back to my room with me... I'll order room service... and we can talk..."

"Okay..." I sighed...

"You look good in jeans..." I breathed as I pulled him into a kiss...

"Thank you..." he breathed. I wanted him to take me to bed and fuck the shit outta me but instead of taking me to bed, he led me to the table and pulled out the chair for me to sit down, so I sat down. Harland went over to the phone and ordered room service... "Yes – I'd like to order breakfast... I'd like the complete breakfast for two... Yes I'd like coffee... 45 minutes... okay..." he said as he hung up, moved down to the edge of the bed, and looked at me...

"You wanted to talk... let's talk..."

"Harland – I'm sorry... I love you so much..." I said as I started crying...

"I love you too... but we're here to talk about my mother..."

"Harland – I tried – but your mother wouldn't stop coming for me..."

"What exactly did my mother do to you?"

"Harland – you know what your mother did to me – why are you asking me that?"

"Answer me... please..."

"It started with what supposed to be our first date – all those comments about my ordering, my drinking, your drinking – then she calls to ask you are you still there, are you still drinking – then she turns on the gps 'cause you turned off your phone – she comes in my house without being invited talkin' about why the fuck didn't you answer your phone – completely ignores me when I ask her to leave – you invite me over for dinner before you sell the house – I pay her a compliment – I tell her the food is really good – she asks me did you really think we would give you nasty food – then she asks me where I think I'm going when I put the dishes in the sink talkin' about we don't leave dirty dishes in the sink in this house – you show her the condo – she tells you you let this Bitch control you 're so knee-deep in my pussy you lost your got-damned mind – you tell her to apologize she says I call it like I see it – then she apologizes the next day like nothing happened – you invite me over for dinner to your condo – we order from Thelma's – after I order my food she tells me I need to eat more vegetables – I tell you I want to give you a massage – she asks me and just where do you think you're giving him a massage at – like you're still a child in her house – then – when I give you a key to my house she askin' why does he need a key to your house if you're movin' in here – then she finds the key – makes a copy of the key – breaks in my house – goes through my closets – and puts on the strap-on talkin' about I see you like big dicks – I know I shouldn't have put that video on live – but I had to stop her..."

"I know my mother put you through a lot – but my mother's not in Facebook – I'm not in Facebook – what were you thinking?"
"I wanted to embarrass her..."
"Did you take it down?"
"Yea..."
"Good..."
"I deposited the check and put the money on my mortgage..."
"What check?"
"The check you got after you sold your house, paid off your condo, paid off your mother's condo, and paid everybody else..."
"Do you still have a balance on your mortgage?"
"I still owe – but $26,000 put a nice dent on the principle..."
"I'm glad..."
"Harland?"
"Yes?"
"Do you think you can forgive me?" I whispered as I started crying. Harland got up, pulled me up out the chair into his arms, and kissed me gently...
"Don't cry..." he breathed as he kissed me again... "I know it wasn't your fault..." he breathed as he kissed me again... "I forgive you..."
Harland..." I cried as he picked me up in his arms, carried me over to the bed, placed me down gently, opened my legs, and got on top of me... "Harland..." I moaned as he began kissing me on my neck. He felt so good I held him tighter as he lifted my shirt and bra up and began sucking on my breast... "Oh Harland..." I moaned as he began

sucking the other one for a few moments and then he took both my breasts in his hands and massaged them as he kissed his way down my stomach... "Harland..." I whispered. He took his hands off my breasts, unbuttoned my jeans, unzipped them, and snatched them off. I kicked off my sneakers and my jeans as he got up on his knees, unbuckled his belt, slid his jeans and boxers off his ass, and put his arms under me to lift me up. He pulled my shirt and bra over my head, eased me back down on the bed, lay down on top of me, and kicked off his jeans and boxers before he entered me... "Oh Harland..." I moaned as he thrust himself in deeper. He covered my mouth with his as he pushed his tongue in my mouth and stroked me slow and deep... and it was driving me crazy... "Mmm... Mmm... Mmm..." I grabbed his ass with my hands and pushed him in deeper as I dug my nails in his ass...

"Mmmph... Mmmph... Mmmph" My orgasm was building like a volcano ready to erupt from within as I moaned in his mouth...

"MMMM! MMMM! MMMM! MMMM! MMMM!"

"MMMPH! MMMPH! MMMPH! MMMPH! MMMPH!" Harland stayed between my legs and we continued kissing until we heard knocking... "Who is it?" he asked...

"Room Service!"

"Oh shit – hold on!" he exclaimed as he jumped up, threw his jeans and shirt on, and answered the door...

"Sorry about that..." he said as he brought the table with breakfast and coffee into the room and closed the door...

"I'll be right back..." I said as I went into the bathroom to wash up. When I came out the bathroom, Harland was sitting at the table smiling at me...

"I'll be right back – have some coffee..." he said as he got up and went in the bathroom to wash up. When he came out the bathroom he sat down and took the covers off the breakfast...

"This looks so good!" I exclaimed...

"They do breakfast right here..." he said as we started eating...

"I love their corned beef hash..."

"I love everything except their yogurt..." he laughed as we finished eating. When we were finished, we both got up and got dressed...

"Come here..." I said as I pulled him close to me... "I wanna take a picture..."

"Are you gonna post it on Facebook?"

"Is that alright?"

"That's fine..." he said as he hugged me and I took the selfie. Harland waited for me to post it and then he took my phone...

"Breakfast with my love..." he read as he smiled...

"You want me to send it to you?"

"No – I'll get it later..."

"Speaking of later – can I see you later?"

"I'll think about it..." he answered...

"What are you doing for the rest of the day?"

"I have some things I need to take care of..."

"Do you need help with the arrangements?"

"No..."

"Okay – I'll give you some time – I love you..." I breathed as I kissed him..."

"I love you too..."

"I'll call you tonight..." I said as I left...

"Hmm – Harland's not answering his phone – okay – I'm going to talk to him in person..." I said out loud as I ordered an uber...

"Harmony – what are you doing here?"

"I told you I was going to call you – you didn't answer your phone..."

"I didn't answer my phone because I don't want to talk to you..."

"Harland – what's going on?"

"Come over here..." he said as he grabbed me by my arm and pulled me away from the door...

"Harland – you're hurting me..."

"I told you don't ever call me again – what part of that don't you understand?!"

"Harland – this morning – you said you forgave me..."

"Harmony – whatever you're smoking – stop – I didn't tell you anything this morning – I didn't see you this morning!"

"Really?!" I snapped as I took my phone out my pocket and showed him my post... "Who's this then?!"

"Hmmm... I see you've met my twin brother, Horace..."

How Far Are You Willing To Go? 3

The phone startled me as usual. I waited until the room stopped spinning and for the pounding in my head to subside as I waited for the answering machine to come on. After the phone rang for the 12th time, I had no choice but to get up and answer it – otherwise I would have had a migraine headache along with my coffee.

"Hello?" I yawned into the phone.

"Hey girl – what's up?"

"Oh hi Char."

"You up for company?"

"Not really."

"Oh."

"Girl you know you can come over here anytime you want too," I laughed.

"But you said you're not up for company."

"I know but that doesn't mean – girl git your ass over here," I laughed before I hung up the phone.

When Char got there she could smell the coffee right away. "Mmm... that smells good – what is it?"

"Hazelnut."

"You got half & half?"

"I got that and Amaretto – which do you prefer?"

"I prefer to stay sober 'till at least 12 noon," she laughed as she followed me into the kitchen. I made 2 cups of coffee, passed one to Char, and we went into the dining room and sat at the table.

"Nothing like fresh brewed coffee to wake up the senses and alleviate stress," I said as I sipped my coffee.

"I'm surprised we don't smoke too," Char said as she sipped her coffee.

"I never did like cigarettes Char."

"Me either Trenice."

"When I was little my Grandma used to always tell me – here – go light this cigarette for me," I laughed.

"I think all grandmothers do that," she laughed.

"Yea – but her cigarette would always go out and she'd tell me I have to pull on it a little bit to keep it lit," I laughed.

"Then Damn! I'm surprised you didn't start sneakin' a cigarette for yourself and smokin' it later," she laughed.

"I never even thought about it Char – but when I made her coffee and started tastin' it I was hooked!" I laughed.

"I hear that – I started drinkin' coffee when I was 12!"

"Me too!" We laughed for a few minutes then Char said, "Well at least we don't have to worry about lung cancer."

"Not at all – we just have to worry about excess weight, irritable bowel syndrome, ulcers, dehydration, and heart palpitations," I laughed.

"Then damn – how you know all that shit?"

"I read it at the doctor's office – caffeine does all that stuff."

"How does it make you gain weight?"

"It doesn't make you gain weight – it messes with your metabolism so you have problems losing weight."

"What about dehydration? How you dehydrated if you drinkin'?"

"The caffeine depletes your bodily fluids quickly – unless you're in the habit of drinkin 8 to 10 glasses of water a day."

"Then damn – maybe we should switch to decaffeinated..."

"Naaa....," we both said in unison.

We both sat at the table and finished the pot of coffee while we watched Jerry Springer and Maury.

"I can't believe those people wanna tell all the world their business," Char laughed.

"Well if they wanna tell it I wanna hear it," I laughed.

"I know one thing – my daughter wouldn't be goin' on no damn TV talking 'bout she slept with over 20 guys and she don't know who her baby daddy is."

"I hear that – bad enough the town know she a hoe – now 600 million people know she a hoe!" I laughed.

"Then they wanna cry and scream – I know they all watch the show – they know the guys gonna call 'em hoes!"

"What gets me is when the momma's come on the show talking 'bout my son this and my son that – they need to be tellin' their son's use a damn condom!"

"Ya know? My momma always told me – if you gonna be a hoe – be a good hoe – use condoms – then you don't show up in the doctor's office or family court and everyone ain't got to know your damn business!" Char laughed. Then she got real quiet.

"Char? What's wrong? Char?"

"I don't believe this fuckin' shit!"

"What Char? Whaatttt!!!"

"I never got pregnant Trenice!"

"And that's a bad thing?"

"No it's not – but he told me he wanted children…"

"I thought you were glad you didn't get pregnant?"

"I am!"

"Then why are you so mad?"

"Cause if I was tryin' to get pregnant and we didn't use nothin' – how the fuck is Sissy pregnant?" I thought about it for a minute…

"Then damn!"

"Now you got it?"

"Ain't this a bitch – the pot callin' the mothafuckin' kettle black!"

"That's what I'm talkin about!"

"Everybody feelin' sorry for Sissy n shit – even me – and she ain't no better than Cornell!" I laughed.

"Well she 'bout to cash in 'cause she got his name and she got pregnant before he died so she'll get survivor benefits for that child along with the other ones."

"I told Jordan she was probably glad he was dead!"

"You did? When did you say that?"

"Before we went to his funeral."

"Oh."

"You really wanted his baby?"

"Yea."

"Damn Char."

"Please don't start Trenice."

"I'm not…but…"

"But what?"

"Well…"

"What Trenice? Just say it dammit!"

"Ok – but remember I love you ok?"

"Of course…now what the hell you wanna know?"

"Have you been tested?"

"I know I'm not pregnant Trenice…"

"That's not what I mean…"

"Yea – I was tested a couple months ago.

"But that was before Char."

"Yea? So?"

"So what if he gave you something Char? You need to get tested again."

"Trenice?"

"Yea?"

"Why did you get tested again?" Shit! I knew she was gonna start on that…

"Don't be tryin' to change the subject missy," I laughed.

"Stop it Trenice."

"Stop what Char?"

"Stop lyin' to me!"

"Char why in the world would I lie to you?"

"You tell me…"

"Tell you what Char? What have I lied to you about?"

"You right Trenice – I shouldn't accuse you of lying."

"Exactly."

"But I know damn well you not telling me everything either."

"Char, you're my best friend."

"I know but…"

"But nothing! You are the only person I confide in and you've never betrayed me…"

"Yes but…"

"There you go buttin' me again! I know we've been friends for a long time and I also know I don't know every intimate detail of your life – and you know what Char?"

"What Trenice?"

"I don't care!"

"Watchumean you don't care?" she asked as she started crying...

"Oh my God Char – what is wrong with you! I never said I don't care about you – I just said I don't care if you don't tell me every little intimate detail of your life!"

"Why?"

"Because some things should stay between you and God, Char."

"Trenice I don't get you..."

"Char!"

"What?"

"How many men have you slept with?"

"That's none of your fuckin' business!"

"Exactly!"

"Huh?"

"Just because were best friends doesn't mean I feel like you're keeping something from me 'cause you won't tell me how many men you've slept with – only you and God know – understand?"

"I guess...but if you really wanna know..."

"No Char – I don't wanna know – ugh!" I said as I threw up my hands in frustration.

"What's wrong with you?"

"Nothing! And there's nothing wrong with you either!"

"Trenice I know what you're up to..."

"Ok detective – what am I up to?"

"You tryin' not to answer my question."

"And what question is that Char?"

"I answered yours…"

"Yes you did – you told me it was none of my fuckin' business!" I laughed.

"So is that how you feel?"

"Watchu mean?" I asked mocking her.

"Do you feel like it's none of my fuckin' business why you got tested again?"

"No Char."

"So answer the question then."

"Why?"

"Why what?"

"Why do you need to know so bad Char? What's bothering you?"

"I don't know…nothing…everything…I don't know!"

"Char?"

"Yea?"

"I got tested again because it was necessary."

"Oh."

"Trenice?"

"Yea?"

"You said you should've told Jordan before…"

"Yea."

"Then you said - how could I do this to him…"

"Yea."

"Then you said you were confused…"

"Yea."

"Then you said you didn't cheat on Jordan…"

"Yea."

We sat in silence for a few minutes.

"I gotta go Trenice – I'll see you later."

"Ok Char," I said to her back as she closed the door behind her.

How Far Are You Willing To Go? 5

When we got to the precinct, Tyler was sitting there with three cups of coffee. "I thought you said you'd be here by 10 a.m.," Tyler laughed.

"What time is it?" Jordan laughed.

"10:15," Tyler laughed.

"Sorry about that man," Jordan said.

"No need to apologize," Tyler laughed. "You're actually early – Detective Rosa won't be here until 10:30," he laughed again. "I actually thought this coffee was gonna get cold," he said as he handed me a cup, and then Jordan.

"Thanks man – you're the best," Jordan said.

"Can I get you to put that in writing?" Tyler asked.

"Absolutely," Jordan said.

"Good morning Mr. Marshall, Mr. Williams, I'm Detective Morack - Detective Rosa is here so we'll be starting shortly – this way please..."

"Good morning Detective," I said sarcastically.

"This way please," he repeated.

"Don't be rude to my wife," Jordan snapped.

"Excuse me?" Detective Morack asked.

"My wife spoke to you," Jordan said.

"I wasn't speaking to her!" he snapped.

"You know what mothafucka?" Jordan asked as he stepped towards him. Tyler pushed Jordan back as Detective Barros came out into the lobby.

"Do we have a problem here?" he asked, looking Jordan directly in the eyes.

"Yea we got a fuckin' problem – my wife said good morning and Detective Morack told me he wasn't speaking' to her!" Jordan snapped. Detective Rosa walked into the lobby.

"Detective Rosa – please take Mr. Williams and his attorney into the first door on the left – Mrs. Williams, I apologize for his behavior – Detective Morack – come with me," Detective Barros said as Detective Morack followed him into the office and slammed the door...

"I'm sick of your shit!" Detective Morack yelled.

"If you're so sick of my shit – put in your fuckin' papers – it isn't my fault or anyone else's that your wife left you – you may have gotten away with that shit in the other precinct but you're not getting away with it here – I have enough complaints in your file to put you on administrative leave – and trust me – you won't get paid – and you won't have to worry about your wife taking your house because you won't have one left for her to take – and if you think I'm playing with you – try me!" Detective Barros yelled. I was stunned. Detective Morack walked out of Detective Barros's office and down the hall right past me and went into the room on the left where Jordan and Tyler were. I didn't have to listen too hard because no one was whispering...

"Is everything okay Mrs. Williams?" Detective Barros asked.

"Yes, I'm okay," I answered.

"Can I get your more coffee?" he asked.

"No thank you – I'm good," I answered.

"Okay then – if you change your mind, just come get me," he said as he went back into his office...

"Thank God," I said out loud as I turned my attention towards the room on the left...

"So when was the last time you saw Dr. Aiden?" Detective Morack asked.

"I don't remember," Jordan answered.

"You're full of shit!" Detective Morack snapped.

"Detective Morack, that isn't necessary," Tyler said.

"He's right," Detective Rosa said.

"Actually, I'm not full of shit – I haven't had breakfast yet," Jordan laughed, "but let me know where the bathroom is in case I need to use it," he laughed again.

"Mr. Williams, this isn't funny," Detective Rosa said.

"The hell it ain't," Jordan said. Tyler put his hand on Jordan's shoulder. "I'm good Tyler," he said, "but this shit here is hilarious – this is worse than an old episode of law and order," he laughed.

"I've had just about enough of you!" Detective Morack yelled.

"Oh so you Robo Cop now?" Jordan laughed. "I could'a wrote a better script then this," he laughed again.

"Mr. Williams – please excuse my partner – something's wrong with him." Detective Rosa said.

"Tell me something I don't know," Jordan laughed.

"You don't know we have video surveillance of you running through the parking lot right before we found Dr. Aiden dead in his car," Detective Rosa said.

"Is that right?" Jordan asked.

"Yes – that's right," Detective Rosa answered.

"Okay...," Jordan said.

"So do you have an explanation for what you were doing in the parking lot?" Detective Rosa asked.

"No I don't – and I don't need one," Jordan answered.

"Yes you do," Detective Rosa said and Detective Morack smirked.

"Why's that?" Jordan asked.

"Because you're a suspect," Detective Rosa answered.

"Because I ran through a parking lot? Get the fuck outta here!" Jordan laughed.

"Because you ran through the parking lot shortly before Dr. Aiden was killed," Detective Morack said.

"You sure about that?" Jordan asked.

"Unfortunately for you... yes," Detective Morack answered. "It's not like anyone would blame you if you did it – after all – we saw what he did to your wife," Detective Morack sneered.

"Lord please...," I started praying, but God was right on it, answering the prayer I started as Jordan spoke...

"Let me tell you something Detective Morack," Jordan said as he stood up. I could see his silhouette through the glass. Tyler tried to pull Jordan back to sit down but Jordan wasn't having it... "If I killed Dr. Aiden – I've worked at that hospital since before you got to this precinct – I know where every camera is – I wouldn't be stupid enough to kill him in the parking lot where I could be seen, and then leave him in his car," Jordan said as he continued to stand.

"I never said you were stupid," Detective Morack sneered.

"You never said you had any evidence either," Jordan said.

"Mr. Williams – you had motive, you had means, and you had opportunity," Detective Rosa said.

"If you were sure about that you'd be placing me under arrest," Jordan said.

"We can arrest you anytime we want," Detective Morack said.

"Tyler, my coffee's wearing off and we haven't had breakfast - I'm ready to go," Jordan said as he got up and started towards the door...

"Mr. Williams we're not done," Detective Rosa said.

"You may not be done, but I am – have a nice day gentlemen," Jordan said as he opened the door and saw me standing there. "You comin' Tyler?" Jordan asked as he put his arm around my waist and pulled me close to him.

"I guess I am," Tyler laughed. "Where are we going?"

"Parkside Diner," Jordan and I said in unison.

"Okay," Tyler laughed. "Oh shoot – that's my phone – I need to take this – I'll meet you outside," Tyler said as he ran out the front door.

"Jordan?" I asked.

"Yes Beautiful?" he answered.

"Never mind," I said.

"Everything okay Mr. Williams?" Detective Barros asked.

"Yes sir!" Jordan answered as he pulled me closer to him.

"Glad to hear it – have a good day," he said as we walked towards the front door.

"Wait a minute Honey," I said as I turned to throw my empty coffee cup away... and watched Detective Rosa hand Detective Barros a tape...

When we got to Parkside Diner we were seated right away. As soon as we got comfortable, I told Tyler and Jordan what I saw. "I saw Detective Rosa pass a tape to Detective Barros."

"When?" Jordan asked.

"When I went to throw my cup away," I answered.

"Muthafuckas!" Jordan exclaimed.

"Don't worry about it," Tyler said.

"Why shouldn't I worry about it?" Jordan asked.

"Because it's procedure," Tyler answered.

"I thought they only did that when you got arrested?" I asked.

"They do that with everyone," Tyler answered.

"Why?" Jordan asked.

"Because of dicks like Detective Morack," Tyler answered. "He wasn't supposed to treat you like that in the interrogating room."

"He wasn't?" Jordan asked.

"Hell no! He went way over the line – especially when he told you he saw what Dr. Aiden did to your wife."

"I caught that," Jordan said.

"I started praying," I said.

"Oh you heard that Trenice?" Tyler asked.

"I heard everything Tyler," I answered.

"Damn – I'm glad I'm on your side – you're dangerous," Tyler laughed. I didn't laugh with him because I didn't think it was funny – true – but not funny. Jordan caught the look on my face and continued.

"Tyler, I'm good at bait," Jordan said.

"What do you mean?" Tyler asked.

"You watch enough episodes of Law & Order, you figure it out," Jordan laughed.

"What did you figure out?" Tyler asked.

"There's a reason you always get questioned at the precinct," Jordan answered. "If they have something on you already, they arrest you. If they don't have anything on you, they try and bait you so you'll flip out or you'll slip up – this way then can arrest you and detain you for 24 hours – this gives them more time to dig."

"Damn – you're even more dangerous than you're wife," Tyler laughed. Jordan didn't crack a smile.

"Here's your coffee," the waitress said when she placed two cups of coffee on our table.

"Would you like coffee as well sir?" she asked Tyler.

"No thank you," Tyler answered.

"Okay – that'll be one short stack with bacon and two eggs medium – don't break the yolk – with corned beef hash and white toast – light with butter – what can I get you sir?"

"I'll have scrambled with sausage," Tyler answered.

"Will that be white, wheat, or rye?" she asked.

"Rye," Tyler answered.

"With home fries or grits, or French fries?" she asked.

"Home fries," Tyler answered.

"I'll be back shortly," she said.

"I'm impressed," Tyler said.

"Yea – we're regulars here," Jordan said.

"I like the waitress," Tyler said.

"So do we," I said.

"Well I'm sure glad that's over," Tyler said. "Me too," Jordan said as the waitress brought our food to the table.

"Can I get you anything else?" she asked.

"No thanks," I said.

"Enjoy your breakfast – and thank you for choosing Parkside," she said as she went to another table.

"I have to admit – I was worried," Tyler said.

"I wasn't worried at all," Jordan said.

"I could tell," Tyler laughed.

"I didn't do anything to be worried about – at least nothing they know if," Jordan laughed.   "Umm… should I be hearing this?" Tyler asked.

"No you shouldn't – you should be hearing the fork hit your plate 'cause this food is slammin'!" Jordan said as we ate.

My Christmas Miracle

Mommy was up early... "Well well – this is a surprise..." Bri said as she came into the kitchen...

"I couldn't sleep so I figured I'd help you cook..."

"Okay – who are you and what have you done with my child?" Bri laughed...

"I can't help it..." Mommy laughed...

"Well thanks – I appreciate it – but don't you think you should've started breakfast before you started dessert?"

"Nope – the cake needs time to cool..."

"You made the cake so you could lick the bowl..." Bri laughed...

"Good morning..." Robert said...

"Good morning Daddy – coffee's ready..."

"Smells good – and I see you made cake..."

"And apple pie..." Mommy said as she took it out the oven...

"Oh wow..." Robert father said...

"I wanted to help Mommy with the cooking..."

"Okay – who are you and where's my child?" Robert laughed...

"I made breakfast too..." Mommy said as she took the biscuits out the oven...

"Okay Cyn – what's going on?" Bri asked...

"I just wanted to help you Mommy..."

"Well thank you – I appreciate it..." Bri said as her parents went to sit down. Mommy put the biscuits in a bowl and put the bowl on the table...

"I'll get coffee..." Robert said...

"Sit down Daddy – I'll get it..." Mommy said as she got two mugs, poured two cups, and placed them on the table in front of her parents...

"Thank you Cyn..." Robert said...

"You're welcome Daddy..." Mommy said as she went over to the refrigerator, took out the cream, and put it on the table...

"If I knew going to meet Ryan's parents for dinner would get you to help out like this – I would've gone to meet them a long time ago!" Bri laughed...

"There ya go..." Mommy said as she put a plate of scrambled eggs with cheese and turkey sausage on the table...

"Scrambled eggs – with cheese?" Robert asked...

"Oh – sorry Daddy – I forgot..."

"Don't worry about it – I'll eat 'em..." he said as he took some eggs and turkey sausage off the plate along with a biscuit...

"This sure smells good..." Bri said as she took some eggs and turkey sausage off the plate along with a biscuit...

"Thanks Mommy..." Mommy said as she took some eggs and turkey sausage off the plate along with a biscuit and started eating. Mommy's parents watched her as she ate...

"Hungry eh?" Bri asked...

"Mmm hmmm..." Mommy nodded as she continued eating. Mommy got up, poured herself some coffee, sat at the table, and watched her parents as they finished eating...

"Cyn – you're drinking coffee..." Bri said...

"Uh huh..."

"You never drink coffee..."

"I had a taste for it..." Mommy said as she finished her coffee... "I'll wash the dishes Mommy..."

"Okay – that's it – what's going on?" Bri asked...

"Bri – leave her alone!" Robert laughed... "She's excited – she made dessert – she made coffee – she made breakfast – she wants to wash the dishes – let her be!"

"Okay Robert... I'll let her be..." Bri said as she gave him the side eye. Mommy got up from the table, got the plates and silverware, and put them in the sink...

"I'll leave the cups in case you want some more coffee..." Mommy said as she turned her back to them and started washing the dishes...

"Robert – let's go in the library..." Bri said as she got up and they both left the kitchen...

"I think Cyn is pregnant..." Bri whispered...

"Are you serious?" Robert laughed...

"I've been watching her closely – she's sleeping a lot, she's eating more – and she never drinks coffee!"

"I love you..." Robert laughed as he kissed her...

"Robert – I'm serious..."

"Bri – you don't remember – do you?"

"Remember what?"

"You don't remember how nervous I was?" he laughed...

"You were a nervous wreck!" she laughed...

"This is a big deal for Cyn..."

"You're right..."

"Ya know..." he said as he moved up behind her... "We have some time before we go over there..." he whispered in her ear as he put his arm around her...

"Robert... stop..." she laughed...

"No..." he breathed as he began kissing her on her neck...

"Oh Robert..." she moaned...

"Come upstairs with me..." he said as he took her by the hand and led her upstairs...

"Mom? Dad?" Mommy called... "Hmmm – I guess they went back to bed – I'm tired – I'ma sit here for a minute..." she said as she sat in her father's chair...

"Oh Robert..."

"Bri..."

"Robert... Robert... Robert...

"Bri... Bri... Bri..."

"I'm cumming Robert..." Robert kissed her to muffle her moans so Mommy wouldn't hear them... "Mmmm... Mmmm... Mmmm..."

"Mmmph... Mmmph... Mmmph..."

"Hey..."

"Hi Ryan..."

"You okay?"

"Yea... I'm just tired..."

"You sure you're okay?"

"Yea – I was up early – I couldn't sleep so I made chocolate cake and apple pie for dessert..."

"Oh wow – you didn't have to do that..."

"I wanted to..."

"I know my Mom will appreciate it..."

"I made breakfast too..."

"Oh wow – I wish I was there..."

"I wish you were here too..."

"We'll see each other soon..."

"My Mom started asking questions..."

"Really?"

"Yea – I made eggs with cheese and I drank coffee..."

"What's wrong with that?"

"I forgot my Dad doesn't like cheese in his eggs and I never drink coffee..."

"Ooohhh..."

"Thank God my father told her to leave me alone..." Mommy laughed...

"Your mother's a detective..."

"Yes she is..."

"Well she'll know in a few hours – they'll all know..."

"Uh huh..." Mommy yawned...

"You should go take a nap..."

"I will – but I'm gonna sit in the library for a while first..."

"Why?"

"Because if I go upstairs now... I'll hear my parents having sex..." Mommy laughed...

"Are you serious?!"

"Yup..."

"How do you know?"

"They don't go upstairs during the day unless they're having sex..."

"Oh wow – that must be awkward..."

"Not really – if I'm in my room I put my headphones on and do school work – If I don't have any work to do I listen to music or I come downstairs to the library..."

"How can you be so cool about it?"

"Well – right now Daddy's keeping her mind off of me..." Mommy laughed...

"Oh Robert... I love you..." Bri breathed as they kissed...

"I love you too..."

"Let's stay here..."

"We can stay here for a while if you want..."

"I'm gonna celebrate when Cyn moves out..."

"Oh yea?"

"Yea..." Bri breathed as she slid down between Robert's legs...

"Got Damn..." he moaned...

"Ssshhh..." Bri whispered as she continued...

Obsidian Heart

"Good morning..." Jade breathed in Sid's ear...

"What time is it?" he groaned as he rubbed his eyes...

"It's a little after 5..." she breathed as she turned him over on his back and began kissing her way down his chest to his stomach...

"Why'd you wake me up... so... early..." he panted as he began playing in her hair as if he didn't know shy she woke him up. This was another pattern between the two of them – Jade knew her husband always woke up with a hard-on – and she also knew he preferred her mouth to a hand job any day – and ever since they said 'I Do' she hasn't missed a day... "Jade..." he moaned as she took his dick in her mouth all the way down to his balls... "Oohh... Shit..." he moaned. This was another pattern between the two of them. Sid knew whenever he was upset with her, she would put it on him good – and this morning, he was ready for it... "Yeesss... Suck it... Shit..." This was music to Jade's ears but unbeknownst to Sid, this morning was going to be a little different... "Why'd you stop?" he asked as he sat up...

"Ssshhh..." she whispered as she pushed him back down on the bed, straddled him, and sat on his dick. Sid was disappointed until she started bouncing up and down...

"Oh Sid... Yes... Fuck me..." Sid grabbed her ass and slammed her down on his dick as he thrust himself up inside her... "Yes... Oh God... Sid... Sid..."

"Ugh! Ugh! Ugh!"

"Sid... I'm cumming... I'm cumming..."

"Ugh! Ugh! Ugh! Ugh!"

"Huh! Huh! Huh! Huh!" Jade lay down on Sid while he was still inside her and kissed him... "I love you..."

"I love you too..."

"You want breakfast before you go to work?"

"Naa – it's early – I'll just take coffee..."

"I'll go make you some coffee..." she said as she got up off him...

"Jade – wait..." he said as he got up out the bed...

"Yes Sid?

"Come take a shower with me..."

"Okay..." Jade was elated that Sid asked her to come shower with him but what she didn't realize was that he asked her to take a shower with him to take his mind off of me...

"Good morning – thank you for calling Heart Tech..." I answered...

"Good morning – may I speak with Mr. Heart please..."

"Hi Mr. Osgood – he's not in yet..."

"Hi Amber – how are you?"

"I'm good – thank you for asking..."

"You're welcome – please have him call me..."

"I sure will – oh wait – he just came in - Mr. Heart – Mr. Osgood is on the phone for you..."

"Thank you – I'll take it in my office..."

"Bazil – what can I do for you?"

"I have a proposal for you Sid..."

"Oh boy – I'm listening..."

"It's not bad!" Bazil laughed...

"Bazil – I know you well enough to know that you don't do anything for anyone out of the kindness of your heart..." Sid laughed...

"Now see – I'm hurt..."

"I'm sorry – go 'head..."

"I told my wife your story..."

"My story?"

"I told my wife about your name, your crystals, and how they've been in your family for generations..."

"Oh boy – she thinks I'm crazy – right?"

"Not at all – in fact – my wife loves crystals..."

"Really?"

"I know – I was just as surprised as you are..."

"Oh wow – how do you feel about that?"

"If my wife told me she loved shit on a stick – I'd go get her some – as long as she didn't bring it in the house!"

"Bazil!" Sid laughed... "I can't!"

"When I died – my wife died – she came after me – she begged God for my life – and here I am – so if crystals make her happy, I'm all for it – which brings me to the reason I'm calling you..."

"Wait – wait – wait – you never told me you died!"

"I'll get back to that another time – let me tell you why I'm calling!"

"Okay, okay!" Sid laughed...

"My wife wants to publish your story..."

"What?!"

"My wife says there are a lot of people that are interested in crystals and she'd love to publish your story..."

"Oh my God – I don't believe it!"

"So are you interested?"

"I need to think about it..."

"Check your email..."

"Why?"

"My wife asked her cover designer to make a cover – take a look at it and then let me know what you think..."

"Okay Bazil – thanks..."

"You're welcome..." Bazil said as he hung up...

"Amber – could you come in here please?"

"Sure Mr. Heart – I'll be right there..." I answered as I got up and went into his office...

"Close the door..."

"I'm not sure that's a good idea – I don't want anyone telling your wife I'm in your office with the door closed..."

"There's no one else here..."

"I'd rather leave the door open..." I said as I went to sit down and he stopped me...

"Wait – come over here – I want to show you something..."

"On your computer?"

"Yes..."

"Okay..." I said as I went behind the desk and bent down... "Oh my God!" I thought to myself as I caught his scent... "What am I looking at?" I asked, snapping myself out of my thoughts...

"This is an email from Beautiful Publications..."

"Beautiful Publications?"

"Yes – that's a publishing company under Osgood Publishing..."

"Oh my God! You're writing a book?!"

"His wife wants to publish my story..."

"Oh Sid – that's great! Congratulations!"

"Thank you..."

"Open it!" I exclaimed...

"Okay, okay!" he laughed as he opened the email and we both looked at the cover...

"Oh my God! That cover is fire!" I exclaimed...

"It is nice..."

"Is that your wife?"

"Yes..."

"How'd they get your picture?"

"Bazil and his wife were at our wedding..."

"Ohhh..."

"He must've given this picture to his wife..."

"His wife owns Beautiful Publications?"

"Yes..."

"Looking at this cover, she makes me want to write a book..."

"Really?"

"Yes!"

"How would you feel about being in this book?"

"Me? Why me?"

"Because..." he said as he stood up... "You're part of my story..." he breathed as he pulled me into his arms and kissed me. I knew I should've pushed him away but he felt so good I didn't want him to stop, so I put my hands around his back as we continued kissing..."

"Sid? Are you here?" Jade called out, startling us both..."

"I'm in here!" Sid answered, giving me time to adjust myself...

"There you are!" she said as she came into the office...

"Hi Mrs. Heart..." I greeted...

"Hello Amber..."

"What brings you down here?" Sid asked as I went to sit back at my desk...

"You left your briefcase at home – I thought you might need it..."

"Thank you – I didn't realize I left it home...

"Have you had lunch?"

"Not yet..."

"C'mon – I'll take you to lunch – my treat..."

"Sounds good to me..." he said as he got up from his desk. I turned to see them walking out of his office holding hands... "Amber – we're going out to lunch – I'll be back later..." he said as they left...

"Thank you Lord..." I sighed...

Obsidian Heart 2

"Good morning My Queen... Sid breathed as he kissed me...

"Is it?" I asked as I got up out the bed...

"I'm..."

"You're sorry – right?!" I interrupted...

"Yes..." he sighed...

"Do you know why you're sorry or do you just say you're sorry out of habit?!"

"Please – let me explain..."

"I swear to God – you better not be telling me you slept with Jade again..."

"This isn't about Jade..." he said as he followed me down the hall to the living room... "This is about me..."

"Let me get some coffee first..." I sighed as I went into the kitchen. Sid watched me make the coffee without saying anything. After I made the coffee, I handed him a cup and sat down next to him...

"I went to see Bazil last night..."

"You said you had to go because you had something to do!"

"I did..."

"What did you have to do with Bazil – especially after we just got home?!"

"I didn't know how to comfort you yesterday..."

"You were comforting me just fine when we were at the hotel..."

"I know – but after Smalls called me yesterday – you got so upset – I tried to apologize – you didn't want to hear it..."

"I don't want to hear you say you're sorry - I want you to hear me!"

"I know that now – and that's why I'm sorry..."

"I don't want to hear it!!" I said as I put my hand in his face and then I pulled him into a kiss...

"I love you..."

"I love you too..." I looked up and noticed the crystals and spheres glowing and spinning... "Sid?"

"Yes My Queen?"

"Where are the gemstones?"

"What time is it?"

"It's 7:30..."

"We need to get ready – we have to be in court by 9..."

"We?"

"Yes..." he answered and then he stood up, took my hand, and pulled me towards the bathroom...

"Good morning..." Smalls greeted...

"Good morning Smalls, good morning Jade..." Sid greeted. Jade didn't respond...

"Good morning..." I sighed as we went inside. I was starting to think I should've just stayed home. When we got in the court room I went to sit in the back...

"Amber – come with me..." Sid said...

"I don't think that's a good idea..." Smalls said...

"Smalls..." Sid started to say...

"It's fine Sid – I'll sit back here..." I sighed...

"Okay..." Sid said as he went to the front of the court room with Smalls and Jade...

After Smalls sat down the Bailiff spoke:

"All rise." We all stood up. "Department One of the Superior Court is now in session. Judge Dulberg presiding. Please be seated."

"Calling the case of Jade Heart versus Obsidian Heart. Are both sides ready?"

"Ready Your Honor..." Sid answered...

"Ready Your Honor..." Smalls said.

"Let's start with the divorce..."

"Your Honor?" Jade asked as she stood up...

"Yes Mrs. Heart?"

"I'd like Amber to leave the courtroom..." she said as she turned and pointed at me...

"Ms. Morrison – please leave the courtroom..." I was already on my way out the door before the judge finished his sentence...

"Let's try this again..." the judge sighed... "We're here to discuss the particulars of the divorce first..."

"Yes Your Honor..." Smalls acknowledged...

"Mrs. Heart – you've agreed to a settlement of $500k, plus alimony of $1,000 a week for 12 years..."

"Yes Your Honor..." Jade acknowledged...

"Mrs. Heart – your husband's company is worth a lot of money – are you sure you want to settle for only $500k?"

"Yes Your Honor..." she answered...

"So noted – now let's settle the custody of your unborn child..."

"That's already been settled..." Sid said...

"Mr. Heart – please refrain from addressing me until you're called to speak..."

"Yes Your Honor..."

"Mrs. Heart – according to this petition – you've agreed to give your husband full custody of your unborn child – is that correct?"

"Yes Your Honor..."

"Would you like to petition the court for visitation at this time?"

"I'm not sure..."

"Very well – I'll enter a judgement granting the divorce between Obsidian Heart and Jade Heart. Custody of the unborn child will be granted to Mr. Heart. Mrs. Heart will be given an opportunity to petition the court for visitation after the child is born..."

"Thank you Your Honor..." Jade said...

"Mr. Heart..."

"Yes Your Honor?"

"You're officially divorced. You've agreed to a settlement of $500k and $1,000 a week in alimony for 12 years. You'll receive full custody of your child – however – Mrs. Heart can petition the court for visitation – and let me make this clear – I will grant her visitation..."

"Yes Your Honor..." Sid acknowledged...

"Smalls – I need to see your client in my chambers..." he said as he got up from the bench and went in his chambers...

"Why does he want to see me in his chambers?" Jade asked...

"I don't know..."

"Can you be in there with me?"

"I can let the judge know you want me to be present if you want..."

"Okay..." Smalls took Jade to the judge's chambers and knocked on the door...

"Your Honor?"

"Yes Smalls – come in..."

"Your Honor – my client has requested that I come with her..."

"Ms. Heart – I'd like to speak with you privately – if you don't like what I have to say – you can leave..."

"Can my attorney wait for me?"

"Absolutely..."

"I'll be in the court room..." Smalls said as he left Jade in the judge's chambers and went back to the court room...

"What's going on?" Sid asked...

"I have no idea..." Smalls sighed...

"Ms. Heart – please – have a seat..."

"Okay..."

"12 years is a long time..."

"Yes Your Honor – it is..."

"Please – call me Joel..."

"Okay... Joel..."

"May I call you Jade?"

"Sure..."

"Jade..." he sighed as he got up, went to sit by her, and took her hand...

"Yes Joel?"

"I want to make your time in prison easier..."

"Easier?"

"I can have you transferred to a section where you can be more comfortable... I want to be able to come visit you... I've grown feelings for you..."

"Are you fucking kidding me?!" she snapped as she pulled her hand away from him...

"Jade – did I say something to offend you?"

"You're offering to make my stay more comfortable – as long as I agree to be your whore – and you don't think that's offensive?!"

"Jade – you have me all wrong..." he said as he got down on bended knee in front of her and took her hand... "I'm not asking you to be my whore..."

"I'm sorry – I just thought – never mind – I feel so stupid..."

"Jade Heart..." he sighed as he reached in his pocket and pulled out a velvet box...

"Oh my God..." she whispered. Joel opened the box and showed her the ring...

"Will you marry me?"

"Are you sure you want to marry me?"

"I've never been more sure of anything in my life..."

"Come sit..." Jade said as she patted the chair. Joel closed the box, got up off his knee, and sat down beside her... "Why me?"

"I've been on the bench for 30 years – I'm not getting any younger – and I'm not trying to meet someone and start dating again just to have my heart broken..."

"How do you know that will happen?"

"I don't – and I'm not trying to find out..."

"Joel – I'm flattered – but I just got divorced – I'm pregnant – I don't know what I'm going to do yet..."

"You don't have to have sex with me if you don't want to – I can wait until you're ready to be intimate..."

"I don't think I'll ever be ready to be intimate as long as I'm in prison..."

"12 years is a long time to be alone... and it's even longer when you're lonely..."

"This is a lot – I had no idea you had feelings for me..."

"I do..."

"How are you going to be able to be a judge and be married to an inmate? What will your colleagues think?"

"I don't give a damn what my colleagues think – once we get married – I'm leaving the bench..."

"You'd leave the bench? For me?"

"If you say yes... then yes..."

"And you're willing to accept my child?"

"Of course..."

"I need to think about this..."

"So... are you saying maybe?"

"I'm saying maybe..."

"Can I kiss you?"

"Yes Your Honor – I mean Joel..." Joel took Jade's face in his hands and kissed her gently and she started crying...

"Please... don't cry Jade..."

"I'm crying because I'm happy..."

"That's fine with me..."

"So how does this work?"

"Well – once you agree to marry me – you come back here – and we can get married in the court room – or in the judge's chambers..."

"You're going to perform your own wedding?"

"No – I'm going to ask Harland Duffey..."

"I still need to think about it..."

"Okay – I'll give you some time..."

"Can I tell Smalls?"

"Not yet..."

"Why?"

"I want you to wait until you say yes..."

"Okay... I'll wait..."

"Can I visit you?"

"Yes Joel..."

"Okay – you can go back in the court room – oh – one more thing..."

"Yes Joel?"

"When we go back in the court room – call me Your Honor..."

"Okay..."

"They've been in there a while now..." Sid said...

"I know..." Smalls acknowledged...

"You sure you don't know what's going on?"

"I have no idea – here they come now..." Smalls said as he stood up a long with Sid...

"Smalls – you can take your client back to prison – have a good day..."

"Thank you Your Honor..." Smalls said as the judge got up and went back into his chambers... "Jade – what was that all about?"

"Nothing..." she sighed...

"Goodbye Jade..." Sid said...

"It certainly is..." Jade sighed as Sid left the court room...

The Ultimate Con

"Good morning..." Aiden yawned...

"What the hell happened last night?" Mary yawned...

"I have no idea..."

"I need coffee..." Mary said as she got up and put on her robe...

"Mary – where are you going?"

"I'm going to the cafeteria to get some coffee..."

"Wait a sec..." Aiden said as he got up... "I'll come with ya..."

"C'mon..." she said as she opened the door and they went out into the hall... "Excuse me..." Mary said...

"Yes?" Harold answered...

"I see you have coffee – do they still have some left?"

"Oh yea – they just made it..."

"Thank you..."

"I'm glad to see you're feeling better..."

"I beg your pardon?" Aiden asked...

"Your wife was being pushed in a wheelchair last night to her room – she didn't look well..." Harold answered...

"Oh my goodness – Aiden – I told you I shouldn't have had any champagne..." Mary laughed...

"I guess not..." Aiden laughed...

"Have a good day..." Harold said as he walked over to the elevator.

"I can't believe I was so drunk I can't remember what happened..." Mary laughed...

"I don't believe it..." Aiden said as they made their coffee...

"Good morning..." Sonovia yawned...

"Good morning..." Flick breathed as he pulled Sonovia into a kiss...

"Uh uh – I'm not doing that again Flick..." she laughed as she got out of bed and went into the bathroom...

"Guess who?" Flick laughed...

"You need to go?" Sonovia asked as she got up off the toilet...

"I need to go – but I need to cum too..." he laughed...

"What time is check-out?"

"12 o'clock..."

"What time is it now?"

"8 o'clock..."

"C'mon..." Sonovia sighed as she took Flick's hand and pulled him out the bathroom...

"Before we shower and get dressed, I wanna go see Flick and Snow..." Aiden said...

"Oh great – I hope we can get them to spend another night..." Mary said...

"I don't care about that – I wanna know what happened last night..."

"Aiden – I got drunk..." Mary laughed...

"I still wanna talk to them..." he said as they left the room and headed upstairs...

"Oh Flick..."

"Snow... Snow... Snow..."

"Flick... Oh shit... Fuck..."

"Okay – we're here – I hope we caught them before they checked out..." Mary said as they headed down the hallway...

"Flick... Don't stop... I'm cummin'..."

"Cum for me..."

"Huh... Huh... Huh... Huh... Huh..."

"Uuugh! Uuugh! Uuugh! Uuugh! Uuugh!"

"I love you..." she panted...

"I love you too..."

"Let's go get in the shower..."

"Okay..."

"Flick? You in there? It's Aiden..." he said as he knocked on the door...

"Maybe they're not in there..." Mary said...

"Flick – I hear somebody knocking..."

"So?"

"Listen – there it goes again..."

"I'll be right back..." Flick sighed as he got out the shower and went to see if anybody was at the door. When he looked out the peep hole, he saw who it was... "Aiden?"

"Yea Flick..."

"We're in the shower – give us a few minutes..."

"Okay – we'll be downstairs – call us when you're ready – I wanna talk to you..."

"Okay..." Flick said as they went down the hall and Flick went back to the bathroom...

"Was somebody at the door?" Sonovia asked...

"Yea – it was Aiden..." he answered as he started washing himself...

"What the fuck? Why are they up here so early?"

"Who knows – he said he wants to talk about last night..."

"Oh shit!"

"What's wrong?"

"Last night somebody saw me pushing Mary in the wheelchair!"

"So what?"

"He asked me if Mary was alright – you think he said something?"

"Baby – you already told the front desk she was drunk – don't worry about it..." he said as he started drying off...

"You right – but why does he wanna talk about last night?"

"Who knows – let's go get dressed so we can get this over with..." he said as he walked into the bedroom and dropped the towel...

"Turn around Baby..." Sonovia commanded...

"Now see... you startin' trouble..." Flick said as he turned around and came towards her...

"I love looking at you naked..." she breathed as she sat down on the bed, grabbed him by his ass, and pushed him in front of her face...

"Snow... they're waiting..."

"Fuck 'em..." she breathed as she took his dick in her mouth...

"Snow... Fuck!" Sonovia loved hearing Flick moan and she began stroking the shaft with her hand while sucking the head of his dick simultaneously... "Snow... Snow... Snow... Oh shit..." Sonovia took his dick all the way in her mouth and when she stroked his balls, he lost it... "I'm cummin'... I'm cummin'... I'm cummin'... UUUGGGHHH!" Sonovia swallowed and continued sucking his dick softly for a few moments until she was sure nothing would drop off her mouth and just as she stopped sucking Flick pulled her up into his arms and kissed her...

"I wanna get back in this bed and fuck the shit outta you..."

"I'll let you make it up to me later – let's get dressed..."

"Okay – I love you..." he said as they started getting dressed. When they were done, she put on a pot of coffee... "They might still have coffee downstairs..."

"That's okay – I'll drink this – you want some?"

"Sure – make me a cup – I'll call them..." Flick said as he dialed their room... "Aiden? It's Flick... Uh huh – come on up..." After he hung up, Sonovia handed him a cup of coffee... "Thanks Babe..."

"You're welcome..." she said as Aiden knocked on the door...

"Aiden?"

"Yea Flick..." Flick got up and opened the door...

"Good morning – come in..."

"Good morning – good morning Snow..." Aiden said...

"Good morning Flick, good morning Snow..." Mary said...

"Good morning guys – did you have breakfast?" Sonovia asked...

"Not yet – my husband wants to talk to you about what happened last night..."

"It was nice until you fell asleep..." Sonovia laughed...

"Did I fall asleep right away?" Aiden asked...

"Naa – we talked about the casino in Queens..." Flick answered...

"We did?"

"Yea – you asked me where I was from – I said Queens – you asked me if they had a casino there – I told you about New Resorts..."

"I don't remember any of that – what the hell's a matter with me?"

"You had a long day yesterday – and a long night – sorry it didn't work out at the tables..."

"I remember that..." Aiden laughed...

"Snow – did you have to push me in a wheelchair?" Mary asked...

"I didn't have to – but you were out of it – I didn't wanna take any chances..."

"Oh my God – was I that bad?"

"No – it wasn't like that – you just fell asleep on the couch – I woke you up – I told you it was time to go to bed, I took you to your room, you got in bed, you went back to sleep..."

"Snow went to sleep on me too..." Flick lied...

"Really?" Aiden asked...

"After I brought you to your room – I came back – she was out!"

"What the hell was in that champagne?" Aiden laughed...

"Snow can't drink wine and champagne together – they both make her sleepy..."

"Oh that's right – we did have wine!" Mary exclaimed...

"I guess Heineken, steak, champagne, and a losing streak didn't do me much good..." Aiden sighed...

"You probably needed the rest – it's a good thing you're staying an extra day..." Flick said...

"I wish you were staying an extra day..." Mary sighed...

"I'm sorry Mary – I can't – I need to get back to work..." Sonovia said...

"You guys wanna go get breakfast?" Aiden asked...

"No thanks – we need to get going..." Flick said...

"Okay – I guess we'll see you next time..." Aiden said as he got up to leave...

"Mary – what's your number?" Sonovia asked as she pulled out her cell phone...

"203-508-2790..." Sonovia put the number in her cell phone and called Mary. Mary looked at her phone... "Is this you?"

"That's me..."

"Okay – I'll save it under Snow..."

"Good – I'll call you later..."

"Okay!" Mary exclaimed...

"Okay Flick – nice meeting you – see you soon..."

"Nice meeting you too..." Flick said...

"We'll see ourselves out..." Aiden said as they left. As soon as they left, Flick went over to Sonovia...

"Why the fuck did you give her your phone number?"

"First of all – don't fuckin' talk to me like that!"

"You right Baby – I'm sorry..."

"Second – Aiden already suspects something – we need to act like we cool..."

"You right Baby – I didn't think about that..."

"C'mon – let's check out before they come back with more questions..." she said as she took the bottle of melatonin out the night stand, put it at the bottom of the duffel bag, packed everything into the duffel bag, and left the room...

"Something's not right..." Aiden said as they went back into their room...

"Aiden – what are you getting at?" Mary asked...

"I know something happened last night..."

"Aiden..." Mary breathed as she went over to him and pulled him into a kiss...

"Mary – something h..." Mary kissed him again and this time Aiden relented and held her against him as he kissed her hard...

"I'm hungry..." she breathed...

"What would you like?" he asked, smiling at her seductively...

"You..."

"Coming right up..." he said as he walked her backwards to the bed. Mary fell back and Aiden fell down on top of her, kissed her, went up under her shirt, and began squeezing her breasts as his cell phone rang...

"Don't answer it..." she breathed. Aiden looked at the phone...

"Shit – I need to take this..." he said as he sat up on the bed. Mary got up in a huff, went into the bathroom, and turned on the shower...

"Hello Sean..."

"Aiden – I need more time..."

"I thought I made myself clear..."

"Something happened..."

"I don't wanna hear it..."

"I had your money..."

"Had?"

"I went to the room with them..."

"You're making excuses..."

"I had a glass of champagne..."

"You had a glass of champagne? Are you telling me you don't have my money because you got drunk?"

"I didn't get drunk – I was drugged..."

"I'm hanging up..." Aiden laughed...

"I'm serious – I woke up in my room the next day – with no memory of what happened the night before – and $45,000 transferred out of my account..."

"Where was it transferred?"

"It was transferred to Webster Bank..."

"Did you say you went to their room?"

"That's what I said..."

"Do you remember their names?"

"Flick... and Snow..."

"I'll give you 48 hours..."

"48 hours? That's not enough time – I need a few days!"

"You have 48 hours..." Aiden said as he hung up... "I knew something happened – and now I know why it happened..." Aiden smiled as he got up and went into the bathroom...

"Aiden! You scared me!" Mary exclaimed...

"Don't be scared..." he breathed as he pulled her into a kiss, picked up her leg, and thrust himself up inside her...

"Aiden... Oh God... Aiden... Fuck me..." Mary moaned as she held onto his back...

"Uugh... Uugh... Uugh... Uugh... Uugh..."

"Aiden... Don't stop... Don't stop..."

"Uugh... Uugh... Uugh... Uugh... Uugh..."

"Aiden... I'm cumming! I'm cumming! I'm cumming!"

"Uuugh! Uuugh! Uuugh! Uuugh! Uuugh!"

"Whoever that was..." Mary panted... "I need to thank them..."

"You should be thanking me!!" he growled as he turned her away from him, bent her over, slammed his dick inside her, and began pounding her from behind...

The Ultimate Con 2

"Good morning..." "Good morning – does anyone need coffee?" Katina asked..."

"We all need coffee..." Beautiee laughed...

"We can go into the other room and you can help yourself if you like..."

"Thank you..." Beautiee said as she got up... "Honey – I'll get your coffee..." she said to Bazil as she started to leave...

"I'll be right back..." Smalls said as he got up and they went into the kitchen area...

"You don't mind leaving your husband alone with Katina?" Smalls asked...

"Naa... I get a kick out of it..." Beautiee laughed as they made their coffee. When they were finished, they brought their coffee back into Katina's office and sat down... "Here..." Beautiee said as she handed Bazil a cup of coffee...

"Thank you..." Bazil said...

"Thank you for coming in..." Katina said...

"You say that as if I had a choice..." Bazil laughed...

"Let me start by saying that I asked you to come in for questioning – you're not under arrest and you're not being charged..."

"Is my client a person of interest?" Smalls asked...

"Yes... and no..." Katina answered...

"Is this conversation being recorded?" Smalls asked...

"Not by me..." Katina laughed. Smalls sat there and smiled. There are cameras as you can see – but that's surveillance – we're not recording anything – but I will be taking notes, just as you'll be taking notes..."

"That's fine..." Smalls said...

"Bazil – I called you down here for questioning because I met with Mary Holloway – and I have additional questions after reviewing her statement..."

"You have additional questions to the questions you were planning to ask me?" Bazil laughed...

"Exactly..."

"This is gonna be good..." Smalls said...

"Mary said before her husband was killed, he told her somebody owed him money and they didn't have the money to pay him. She also said while they were at dinner, her husband received a call and he was happy because he was told he would be getting paid..."

"Do you have a question for my client?" Smalls asked...

"Yes I do..."

"Okay – go ahead..."

"Bazil – we've reviewed the surveillance videos from Mohegan Sun and we saw you with Sean Stewart..."

"That's not a question..." Smalls said...

"Did Sean Stewart tell you he owed Aiden Holloway money?" Bazil looked at Smalls. Smalls nodded...

"Yes..." Bazil answered...

"I wanna show you something..." Katina said as she put her laptop on the table so everyone could see it... "This is the surveillance of you and Sean... here's where you're following Sean and Aiden to the men's room... you're listening at the door... and then you back away from the door right before Aiden comes out..."

"Do you have a question for my client?" Smalls asked...

"Yes I do..."

"Go ahead..."

"Did you set Sean up to be killed?"

"No..."

"Why were you listening to what was going on in the men's room?" Bazil looked at Smalls. Smalls nodded...

"I wanted to make sure Sean was okay..." Bazil sighed...

"I want you to have another look at this surveillance..." Katina said as she rewound it and played it back. This time, Katina zoomed in on Bazil's face... "You were hurt..." she said...

"Do you have a question for my client?" Smalls asked...

"Yes I do..."

"Go ahead..."

"Did you know what was going to happen in the men's room?"

"No..."

"Did you see where Aiden went when he came out the men's room?"

"No..."

"So – to be clear – you don't know what happened in the men's room?"

"I don't know what happened – but I heard something..." Smalls looked at Bazil and raised his eyebrow...

"What did you hear?"

"When Aiden came out the men's room he called Sean a stupid mother fucker..."

"How did you know Sean owed Aiden money?"

"He told me..."

"So you knew Sean?"

"He was my friend..."

"I'm sorry..."

"Thank you..."

"Did you see where Aiden went after he came out the men's room?"

"No..."

"I have another video I'd like to show you..." Katina said as she played the surveillance showing Bazil leaving the casino with Sonovia... "Who is this woman?"

"That's Sonovia Alexander..."

"How do you know her?"

"What does that have to do with anything?" Smalls asked...

"I'm getting to that..." Katina answered...

"She's an author. She introduced herself to me and told me she's read some of my books..." Bazil answered...

"I wanna show you another video..." Katina said as she played more surveillance... "This is you... going into Foxwoods with Sonovia..."

"Do you have a question for my client?" Smalls asked...

"Not yet...." she said as she played another video... "This is you... leaving Foxwoods..."

"Do you have a question for my client?" Smalls asked...

"Not yet..." she said as she played another video... "This is the surveillance from where Aiden Holloway was killed..." Katina said as she showed zoomed in on the killer's foot... "As you can see – we have no idea who the killer is – all we got on surveillance is his shoe..."

"Do you have a question for my client now?" Smalls asked...

"Yes I do..."

"Finally! Go ahead!"

"Bazil – what size shoe do you wear?"

"I wear a man's 9..."

"May I take a look at your foot?"

"Would you like me to put it up on the table for you?"

"That won't be necessary..." Katina said as she started playing another video...

"What's this?" Smalls asked...

"This surveillance shows you and Sonovia's husband going into Foxwoods the next morning..." Katina pointed out... "And surveillance shows Bazil leaving the casino by himself..."

"Do you have a question for my client?" Smalls asked...

"I have a few questions..."

"Go ahead..."

"Do you know why Sonovia left her husband to go with you?"

"I can't swear to it... but I would say she came with me because she wanted to..." Katina looked at Beautiee. Beautiee looked at Katina and smiled...

"Did you spend the night with her?"

"No..."

"So you went home?"

"I went home..."

"Beautiee – is that true?"

"Absolutely..." Beautiee sighed...

"What made you go back to Mohegan Sun, pick up her husband, and bring him to Foxwoods?"

"It was the least I could do..."

"I don't understand..."

"I would be livid if my wife left me in the casino and went off with another man – I'd want answers – and I'd want the man she left with to answer them..."

"Hmmm... I see..." Katina said as she sat there thinking and tapping her pen on her legal pad...

"Do you have any other questions for my client?" Smalls asked...

"Yes I do..."

"Go ahead..."

"Did you see Mary at the casino?"

"No..."

"Have you seen Mary since her husband was killed?"

"Yes..."

"When did you see her?"

"I saw her yesterday..."

"So you met with her..."

"I didn't meet with her – she showed up at my office..."

"You had no idea she was coming to see you?"

"No..."

"Hmmm... interesting..." she said as she sat there thinking and tapping her pen on her legal pad again...

"Do you have any more questions for my client?" Smalls asked...

"Yes I do..."

"Go ahead..."

"What did Mary want to see you about?"

"She told me everything you discussed..."

"Could you be more specific?"

"Mary told me you questioned her about Sean, her husband, me, and she let me know you had the surveillance..."

"Did she accuse you of killing her husband?"

"No – in fact, she told me she knew I didn't kill her husband..."

"She said that? Those were her exact words?"

"Yes..."

"Hmmm... interesting..." she said as she sat there thinking and tapping her pen on her legal pad again...

"What are you thinking Katina?" Smalls asked...

"Mary told me that they sold you the building where your publishing company is located in Milford..."

"That's correct..." Bazil said...

"So when you saw Mary yesterday – that was the first time you've seen her in about 10 years..."

"That's correct..."

"Hmmm... interesting..." she said as she sat there thinking and tapping her pen on her legal pad again...

"What's so interesting?" Smalls asked...

"I'm going to show you something..." Katina said as she pulled up another video...

"What's this?" Smalls asked...

"This is Mary checking out at 12 the next day..."

"What does that have to do with my client?" Smalls asked...

"I think somebody made sure your client showed up to the right place... at the right time..."

"What?"

"Your client hadn't seen Mary in nearly 10 years... he shows up at the casino... Mary's at the casino... her husband's at the casino... your client's friend is killed... her husband is killed... she doesn't check out until the next day..."

"What does that have to do with my client?"

"Somebody wanted to make it look like your client set this up... somebody wanted us to look at your client... if my husband was killed – I wouldn't be able to sleep – I'd be at the police station..."

"What are you saying?" Smalls asked with a smile...

"Bazil – would you be willing to do something for me?" Bazil looked at Smalls...

"That depends on what you want my client to do..."

"If Mary contacts you again – let me know..."

"Why would my client do that?"

"Never mind..." Katina said as she put her pen in her jacket, closed the laptop, and got up from the table...

"Did I do something to offend you?" Smalls asked...

"No – not at all..." she answered as she picked up the laptop, picked up the notepad, put them in her desk drawer, and locked it...

"Do you need my client for anything else?"

"No – thank you for coming in – have a good day..." she said as she left her office in a hurry...

"What was that all about?" Beautiee asked...

"Not here..." Smalls said as he got up, they got up, and they followed Smalls outside...

"I'll call you later..." Smalls said as he got in his car and left...

Thirst Quencher

"Shit!" LaShonda exclaimed as the water started running out the toilet and onto the floor...

"What's wrong?!" Fritz exclaimed as he jumped up outta bed...

"The fucking toilet's clogged!" LaShonda yelled...

"Move!" Fritz commanded as he pushed LaShonda out the way and dropped down on his knees...

"What are you doing?!" Fritz ignored her question and turned off the valve behind the toilet...

"Thank you..." LaShonda breathed...

"You're welcome – get me a bucket and some towels..."

"Okay – I'll be right back..." she said as she hurried into the kitchen, got the bucket from under the sink, and ran back to the bathroom...

"Where's the towels?"

"I'll be right back..." she said as she hurried over to the linen closet and pulled out as many towels as she could hold and then she handed them to Fritz...

"I'll clean this up – you call the plumber..."

"Okay..." she said as she went to go call the main office...

"Front desk..."

"This is Mrs. Aubert..."

"Yes Mrs. Aubert – what can I do for you?"

"Do you have a plumber available?"

"We have the suppa – what seems to be the problem?"

"Our toilet's clogged..."

"Have you shut off the valve in the back?"

"My husband did..."

"Okay – I'll send the suppa right up..."

"Thanks – but I think we need a plumber..."

"We'll send the suppa first – if he can't fix it then we'll get a plumber..."

"I think I should just get a plumber..."

"That's fine – but I have to inform you that you'll be responsible for any damages to other tenants..."

"What if there are damages from the suppa?"

"There won't be – trust me..."

"Okay..."

"Shall I send him up?"

"Please..."

"Okay – I'll send him right up..."

"Did you call the plumber?" Fritz asked as he came out the bathroom...

"The front desk is sending the suppa..."

"I hope he can fix this..." Fritz sighed...

"I'll go make coffee..." LaShonda said as she went into the kitchen...

"Who is it?" Fritz asked...

"Suppa..." Fritz opened the door and looked him up and down...

"Good morning – my name is Earl..." he said as he extended his hand...

"Mr. Aubert..." Fritz said as he shook Earl's hand...

"I'm here to fix your toilet – may I come in?"

"Yes – of course..." Fritz said as he opened the door...

"Good morning..." LaShonda said as she came into the living room with two cups of coffee...

"Good morning Mrs. Aubert – that coffee sure smells good..."

"Would you like some coffee?" she asked as Fritz rolled his eyes...

"Let's find out what's going on with your toilet..." Earl said as he went into the bathroom with his tools. Once he got in the bathroom he pulled his snake out and proceeded to run it down the toilet...

"How's it going?" Fritz asked as he came in to observe...

"I'll let you know in a sec..." Earl gritted as he pushed the button to reverse so it would come out the toilet...

"What the hell is that?" Fritz asked as he looked at what appeared to be white rocks at the end of the snake...

"Oh my God! What the hell is that?" LaShonda asked as she came to the bathroom...

"Condoms..." Earl answered...

"Condoms? What the hell are they doing in my toilet?" Fritz asked...

"Well Mr. Aubert... that's where they go when you flush them..." Earl answered...

"That's odd – I don't use condoms..."

"You don't?"

"Nope..."

"Well... they could've come from the tenants upstairs – but one thing you should never do is flush condoms down the toilet – it's considered kryptonite to plumbing – especially in apartment complexes..."

"Oh wow..." Fritz said...

"When you flush condoms down the toilet they form giant balls – like the ones you saw – they trap odors and create massive blockages in pipes, plumbing, and sewers..."

"So you should throw condoms in the garbage?" LaShonda asked nervously...

"Absolutely – I'm going to make sure your toilet is working properly before I leave – and then I'll go upstairs and check their toilet..." Earl said as he went back to work...

"I'm going out for a minute – I'll be right back..." Fritz said as he went out the door...

"Mrs. Aubert – you're all set..." Earl said as he came out the bathroom..."

"Thank you Earl..." LaShonda sighed...

"You're welcome..."

"Can I give you a cup of coffee to go?"

"Sure – thank you..."

"I'll be right back..." she said as she went into the kitchen. Earl waited for her to come back with the coffee and when she did, he took a sip right away... "Good huh?"

"Very..." Earl acknowledged...

"Have a good day..."

"You too – and thanks again..." Earl said as he left their apartment and ran right into Fritz... "Oh my God – I'm so sorry!" he exclaimed...

"Don't worry about it – listen – I need to go with you when you check the apartment upstairs..."

"I can't let you do that Mr. Aubert – I could lose my job..."

"Please – I think my wife's cheating on me..." Fritz sighed...

"Oh my God... I'm sorry..."

"So am I..."

"I'll tell you what – you come upstairs with me – if they're home I'll tell them I need to check their bathroom because you're on the same line..."

"What if they're not home?"

"I'll let you know what I find..." Earl said as they both went upstairs. When they got upstairs, Earl knocked on the door...

"We have a problem..." Sterling read the text message and sat with the phone in his hand for a few moments before he replied...

"Who is this?"

"LaShonda..."

"Why are you texting me?"

"The suppa just left here..."

"And you're telling me this because?"

"I'm telling you this because our toilet was clogged from the condoms you flushed..."

"Are you sure it was me?"

'My husband doesn't use condoms..."

"Are you sure it was me?"

"You're the only other man I've been with..."

"I'm sorry about your toilet..."

"We'll have to come up with an alternative..."

"An alternative?"

"For when you come see me next week..."

"Are you fucking crazy?!"

"What's wrong?"

"I'm engaged to Lexi..."

"So what?"

"So you really think I'm going to fuck you ever again in life?"

"That's exactly what I think – in fact – that's what's going to happen – it'll be your gift to me..."

"My gift to you? For what?"

"For not telling your fiancée..."

"Haah! She already knows!"

"You're lying!"

"You wanna talk to her?"

"I wanna talk to you... and then I want you to fuck me... without a condom..."

"Okay – I'll fuck you..."

"Thank you – shall I see you next week?"

"You won't see me at all – but what you will do is continue to pay me – it'll be my gift to you..."

"How the fuck is that a gift to me?"

"As long as you continue to pay me... I won't tell your husband..."

"I'm not paying you shit!"

"Fine with me – oh – before I forget – thank you for our engagement party! Aaah Haah!"

"Fuck you mutha fucka!"

"Mr. Carpentier – I need to check your toilet..." Earl said as Mr. Carpentier opened the door...

"Mr. Aubert – what are you doing here?" Mr. Carpentier asked...

"Our toilet was clogged earlier from condoms being flushed..." Fritz answered...

"Condoms? Well they didn't come from me – my wife and I are trying to have a baby..."

"Congratulations..."

"Thank you..."

"Mr. Carpentier – can I come in and check your toilet?" Earl asked...

"As long as you're not accusing me of causing trouble..." he laughed...

"I'm not – it's just that you're on the same line..."

"Sure – c'mon in..." Mr. Carpentier said as he opened the door and they both went inside...

"Is your wife at home?" Fritz asked as Earl headed to the bathroom...

"No – she gets up and out early..."

"Where does she go so early?"

"She likes to go for a run on the path before it gets crowded..."

"Oh wow..."

"Mr. Carpentier – you're all set..." Earl said as he came out the bathroom...

"Did you find any condoms?"

"I didn't find anything but water..." Earl answered as he headed towards the door...

"Have a nice day..." Mr. Carpentier said as he held the door open for them to leave...

"You too..." they both said in unison as they left...

"Where'd you go?" LaShonda asked as Fritz came in the door...

"I went for a walk on the path..." Fritz lied as he walked past her, sat down at the desk, and started going through the mail. LaShonda shrugged her shoulders and went into the bedroom...

Thirst Quencher 2

"People keep asking 'bout this glow I seem to have 'cause I'm just not the same..." she sang as she pulled the vacuum out of the closet... "They say I'm walking different, talking different, looks like all of me has changed..." she sang as she plugged in the vacuum and turned it on... "Magic is in my eyes..." she sang as she started vacuuming... "I can no longer hide..." she sang as she opened the door to the bedroom to vacuum... and screamed... "AAAGGGHHH!"

"What's wrong?" I yelled as I jumped up off the bed, the sheet fell to the floor, and I stood there in all my glorious splendor, waving my morning erection at Jill...

"Oh my God... I'm sorry... please... excuse me..." she stammered as she backed out of the room...

"Jill?" I called out as I got my robe out of the closet and put it on...

"Yes Mr. Aubert?"

"Wait a minute..." I said as I came out into the living room...

"I'm so sorry – I usually come by once a week to clean – I didn't know you'd be here..."

"Jill... relax..."

"Umm... I really should be going... the bathroom is already clean..." she said as she started to head towards the door...

"Jill..." I said as I reached out and touched her shoulder...

"Umm... Mr. Aubert..."

"Please... sit..."

"Okay..." she sighed. I could tell she was nervous because she kept fidgeting and looking around...

"Hmm... I don't see any coffee..." I said as I looked through the cabinets...

"It's in the fridge..."

"The fridge?" Why would anybody put coffee in the fridge?" I asked as I took the coffee and creamer out the fridge and put it on the counter...

"It keeps the coffee fresher longer..."

"Really? Hmm - I'll have to tell Shonda..." I couldn't believe I just spoke her name...

"Mr. Aubert – if you don't mind..."

"Actually – I do..." I interrupted...

"Mr. Aubert..."

"Fritz..."

"I can't do that..."

"You can't call me by my name?"

"The company doesn't want us to call clients by their first name...

"Would you like some coffee?" I asked, completely ignoring what she said...

"Sure..."

"I'll make it light and sweet – is that alright?"

"Yes Mr. Aubert – I mean Fritz – that's fine..." I smiled when I heard her call me Fritz. I made two cups of coffee, brought them into the living room, put one cup in front of her on the coffee table, and sat down beside her as I started drinking my coffee... "Thank you..."

"You're welcome..."

"I'm really sorry about earlier – it's just that the employees are usually at work during the day..."

"You don't have to apologize – I forgot to put the chain on the door..."

"I guess you had a late night and decided to stay here instead of going home?"

"Sigh... I don't have a home..."

"Oh my God – I'm sorry – I didn't mean to pry – it's none of my business..."

"Last night – I found out I've been a fool..."

"Oh no – that's not true – I'm you're your wife loves you..."

"I wish she did..." I sighed...

"Trust me – she loves you – I've seen how she looks at you..."

"I trusted her – and she cheated on me..."

"Oh no! I'm sorry!"

"So am I..." I sighed as I finished my coffee...

"Is there a chance you can work things out?" Jill asked as she finished her coffee and put the cup on the table...

"I've been a fool long enough..." I said as I got up, picked up the cups, and took them in the kitchen. When I turned around, I didn't realize how close Jill was and before I could say anything, she pulled me into a hug... and it felt good...

"Listen to me..." she said as she held me close to her by my waist... "You're nobody's fool – you're a good man – and you deserve better..."

"That's kind of you to say..." I said as I looked in her eyes. I wanted to kiss her so bad – but the voice of reason was loud and clear...

"Here..." she said as she slipped her card in my pocket...

"What's that?"

"My cell..." she answered before she let go of me, headed towards the door, opened it, and left...

Twisted Beautiee

I was in complete awe as I walked in. "Welcome back Mr. Osgood," someone greeted.

"Sam – how many times do I have to tell you..."

"Welcome back Bazil," Sam said as he grabbed Bazil into a hug.

"This is my wife, Beautiee..." Bazil said as he introduced me.

"Wife? What? – I mean – hell – congratulations!" Sam said as he grabbed me into a hug...

"Thanks..." I laughed.

"Oh – my bad – I'm sorry..." he laughed as he let me go...

"Honey... who's this?" she asked playfully as she walked up towards me...

"I'm Bazil's wife, Beautiee..." I smiled.

"Wife? What?" she said as she grabbed me into a hug...

"Ummm... thank you... who are you?" I laughed.

"Oh... I'm sorry.... I'm Joselyn, Sam's wife, Sam's assistant, and Bazil's 2nd assistant," she laughed as she let me go...

"I guess I got my answer..." I laughed.

"Umm... what was the question?" another lady laughed as she walked up to me...

"Well – I was nervous about meeting you all but I can see I had nothing to worry about," I answered.

"Well who are you?" the lady laughed.

"Mother – that's Bazil's new wife, Beautiee," Joselyn answered.

"Oh my God – congratulations – Bazil – you didn't tell me you were seeing anyone!" she laughed as she hugged me...

"I wasn't aware I had to..." Bazil laughed.

"And who are you?" I asked as everyone got quiet...

"Well... since you asked... I'm Sheila. I'm the Chief Financial Officer. This is the Vice President, my son-in-law, Samuel, and this is his wife, my daughter, Joselyn."

"Well it's lovely to meet you Sheila," I said. Bazil stood to the side beaming with pride and I continued with Sheila as I observed another woman walking up on the conversation... "Bazil and I met a little over a week ago...

"A week ago?"

"Yea..."

"Oh I need to hear this... Bazil, we'll be back – we're going for coffee – come with me Beautiee – you too Joselyn – oh hi MaryJane – this is Beautiee, Bazil's wife – we're going for coffee – you wanna join us?"

"No thank you – nice meeting you though..." she said as she turned to walk towards Bazil and Sam...

"We'll stop in the cafeteria – they make good coffee here," Sheila said as I followed them through the glass doors...

"How do you like your coffee?" Joselyn asked as I sat at one of the tables...

"Hazelnut flavor, hazelnut creamer, light and sweet," I answered.

"Just how Bazil likes 'em..." Sheila laughed as Joselyn walked off to get us coffee... "So tell me how this happened..." Sheila said.

"Well, I met Bazil about a week ago at the Hotel Zero Degrees in Stamford. I was having a drink, he came up to get a drink, we started talking, we hit it off..."

"Hit it off?" Sheila asked...

"Yea..." I answered as I started drifting off...

"Here's your coffee Beautiee," Joselyn said as she sat down with us.

"Beautiee was telling me she met Bazil at the Hotel Zero Degrees a week ago," Sheila said as we started drinking our coffee...

"It happens Ma – you know me and Sam..."

"Yes Joselyn – I know, I know," Sheila laughed.

"Well I don't know – tell me," I laughed.

"I knew I was gonna marry Sam the moment I met him – I didn't know when – but I knew it..." Joselyn answered.

"I had no idea I was getting married – I still can't believe he asked me that night..." I sighed...

"That night? At the hotel?" Sheila asked...

"Well... technically... it wasn't until the next day... before checkout..." I sighed...

"Oh wow..." Joselyn sighed...

"So he met you at the bar... y'all spent the night together... and he proposed the next morning?" Sheila asked...

"Well... technically it was the afternoon... we had a late check out..." I sighed as I drifted off again...

"Well I like you already – you have a nice spirit," Sheila said.

"Awww... thank you..." I said with tears in my eyes...

"You're welcome – so are you going to be working here with Bazil?" she asked.

"Yes I am..." I answered.

"Oh boy – does MaryJane know that?" Joselyn asked.

"I'm sure she does now..." Sheila answered... "And if the doesn't, she goin' learn taday!" she laughed.

"Who's MaryJane?" I asked...

"She's the one who I invited to come get coffee – I knew she wasn't coming anyway – with her stank ass!" Sheila laughed.

"Ma!" Joselyn exclaimed.

"Please Joselyn – you could do her job better – she walks around here like she owns the place... and Bazil..." Sheila said as we continued to sip on our coffee...

"Oh I forgot – I need to get them stats done – le'me run to the bathroom right quick before I miss the deadline," Joselyn said as she darted out of the cafeteria...

"I might as well go to the bathroom – you can make that the 2nd room on the office tour," I laughed.

"Okay – follow me..." Sheila said as she got up and I followed her to the bathroom...

"Oh my God – why?" I heard Joselyn ask...

"She may be nice... for now... until she gets comfortable... then she'll start thinking she runs shit... and I'll have to check her... just like I had to check Janet," I heard MaryJane say. Sheila and I looked at each other and then we both looked back towards the bathroom door...

"You ain't right MaryJane..." Joselyn said.

"Please Joselyn... I've been here for too long to let a Bitch come up in here and knock me outta my position..."

"What position? Your job?"

"That's only part of it..."

"What else is there?"

"She won't last... she may be his wife... for now..."

"What's that supposed to mean?"

"It's only temporary Joselyn," MaryJane answered as she snatched the bathroom door open to exit... and ran right into me...

"Hello MaryJane," I said deliberately as she tried to pass me without excusing herself...

"Oh... Hello Beautiee..." she said...

"Mrs. Osgood," I said, correcting her.

"Excuse me?" MaryJane snapped...

"Please call me Mrs. Osgood," I said as I walked past her, went into the stall, and closed the door. When I came out the stall and went to wash my hands, Sheila spoke...

"Are you okay Beautiee – I mean Mrs. Osgood?"

"Yea... I made it without incident," I answered purposely changing the subject as I washed my hands...

"Ummmmm... I'ma go now..." Joselyn said as she left the bathroom and Sheila followed behind her. I stood there taking my time drying my hands as they spoke on the other side of the door... "Ma... did she hear what MaryJane said?"

"We both did," Sheila answered. I opened the door and walked out into the hallway...

"Sheila, could you please escort me back to my husband's office?"

"Yes Mrs. Osgood – I'll see you later Joselyn," she said as we walked away. I was seething and Sheila knew it, but she didn't say anything as we walked towards Bazil's office...

Twisted Beautiee 3

"Good morning – Osgood Publishing – how may I help you?"

"Good morning Joselyn," I said.

"How are you Mrs. Osgood?" she greeted.

"Not too good – I need you to set up an emergency meeting with the Board of Directors – let Samuel know everyone needs to drop everything – I'll be there at 10," I said as I started getting dressed.

"I'll get right on it Mrs. Osgood – see you at 10."

"Good morning," I greeted as I walked into the Board Room and headed to the head of the table. Thank you all for coming – I'll get right to it. Last night, my husband was shot. He was rushed into emergency surgery at Milford Hospital..." I paused to gather myself as everyone gasped and whispered. I waited for the room to quiet down before I continued... "He came out of surgery but, unfortunately... he's in a comma. At this time, we don't know if he's going to make it..." I paused again to keep from crying and to also give everyone in the room time to adjust to hearing the devastating news... "Effective immediately – Samuel Logan, Vice President, will be acting President and CEO. Everything goes through him and, in turn, he will run everything by me. If there's an emergency and I cannot be reached, Samuel has the final say. Are there any questions?" I asked as Sheila Henley, CFO (Chief Financial Officer) walked in...

"Sorry I'm late..." she said as she closed the door... "What'd I miss?"

"You're fired." I stated. Everyone gasped.

"Excuse me?"

"You're fired – clean out your desk – you have one hour." Sheila exited the room in a huff, closed the door, and I continued... "Are there any questions?" No one answered. Some of the board members acknowledged what I said by shaking their head no. "Very well – thank you for coming." The board members filed out one by one. After everyone left the room, Samuel spoke...

"Mrs. Osgood?"

"Yes Samuel?"

"If you don't mind... I'd like you to reconsider your decision to fire Sheila..."

"Why?"

"We need her... she can't be easily replaced..."

"Are you saying you can't do her job in the interim?"

"I could... it's just that the quarterly reports are due and we have a responsibility to the shareholders..."

"My husband could die at any moment – and I'm here – do you really think I don't know we have a responsibility to the shareholders?"

"You're right – I'm sorry..."

"Go get Sheila," I commanded...

"Yes Mrs. Osgood..." Samuel said as he went to get Sheila..."

"Yes Mrs. Osgood?" Sheila sniffed as she sat down. I looked at her and I could tell she'd been crying...

"What's going on with you?" I asked.

"I'm sorry Mrs. Osgood... my kids..."

"Let me stop you right there!" I snapped. My husband is in the hospital in a comma – he may not make it – and I'm here – do you understand what I'm saying?"

"Yes Mrs. Osgood... sorry about your husband..."

"Samuel asked me to reconsider my decision to fire you because you're valuable and can't be easily replaced," I said as I looked at Samuel...

"Thank you Sam," she said.

"Here's what I need you to do – go home – handle whatever it is you need to handle – and come back tomorrow – but I need you to understand if life happens and you have an emergency – you are to notify us as soon as possible so we are aware – and don't ever walk in late to a board meeting again and ask what'd I miss – is that understood?"

"Yes Mrs. Osgood."

"Okay Sheila – see you tomorrow..."

"Mrs. Osgood..." Joselyn huffed out of breath as she ran into the conference room...

"Yes Joselyn – what's wrong?"

"The police are here – they asked me where you were..."

"It's okay Joselyn – get Attorney Smalls on the phone – have him meet me at the station – tell him I'm being arrested!" I yelled as Joselyn hurried... "Yes Mrs. Osgood!" she yelled as she ran down the hall...

"Mrs. Osgood?" Katina said as she walked over to me with Sergeant Chandler...

"I am..." I said as I stood up...

"We need you to come with us..." Katina said as she went to grab me by the arm...

"Excuse me!" I said as I snatched my arm away from her...

"Mrs. Osgood... please..." Sergeant Chandler asked...

"You said you need me to come with you – I'm quite capable of walking by my damn self!" I snapped as they escorted me out to the squad car.

"This way please," Katina ordered as I was escorted into the Milford City Police Department in Milford, Connecticut.

"How romantic..." I sighed.

"Excuse me?" Katina snapped...

"Well..." I laughed, "When my husband comes out of his comma... we'll be celebrating a few things... one of which will be that we both got arrested... by you!" I laughed hysterically...

"I can't wich y'all – somebody get her and process her..."

"Umm... Detective?" I asked, getting her attention...

"Yes?"

"I am under arrest... right?"

"That's correct..."

"Well..."

"What is it Mrs. Osgood?"

"Are you going to Mirandize me?"

"Oh God... is it 5:00 yet?" she sighed...

"It's always 5:00 somewhere," I laughed, enjoying the fact that she was annoyed...

"Beautiee Osgood... I'm placing you under arrest..."

"Hot Damn! What are the charges?"

"You're being charged with the attempted murder of Bazil Osgood, the murder of Sonia Santos, and the murder of Trevor Joseph…"

"Awww Shit! A Trifecta! Ahhh! Haaa! Haaa!" I laughed…

"What's going on here?" Sergeant Chandler yelled as he came down the hall…

"She thinks this is a fuckin' joke!" Katina snapped…

"That's it – get your ass over here," he said as he came towards me…

"You put your fuckin' hands on me and I'll bury your ass!" I screamed…

"Oh so you gangsta now?" he laughed…

"She's not – but you already know I am," Attorney Smalls said as he walked in…

"Look Smalls," Sergeant Chandler said…

"I'ma need you to step away from my client… have you been Mirandized yet Beautiee?"

"I was trying to do that but your client thinks this is a fuckin' joke!" Katina snapped.

"She's right – it is!" Attorney Smalls laughed, "But you don't need me to remind you that if you don't Mirandize her, you're violating her rights… and I get paid by the hour… so what we doin'?"

"Sigh…" Katina breathed as she began to give me the Miranda warning:

1. You have the right to remain silent.
2. Anything you say can and will be used against you in a court of law.
3. You have the right to an attorney.
4. If you cannot afford an attorney one will be provided for you.

5. Do you understand the rights I have just read to you?"

"I do," I said as I tried to take her hand but she snatched it away...

"With these rights in mind, do you wish to speak to me?"

"Hell no!" Attorney Smalls laughed before I could answer...

"C'mon..." Katina said as she took me for processing. Attorney Smalls met me in the attorney/client room afterwards...

"Beautiee... we need to talk..."

"I know..." I said as I sat down...

"These are some serious charges..."

"I know..."

"I'll defend you with everything I have – but I need to know everything..."

"I know..."

"This is serious... you makin' a joke out there..."

"I laugh to keep from crying..." I interrupted.

"Are you okay?"

"Hell no!"

"You need anything?"

"I need a drink..."

"The best I can do is coffee – I'll be right back," he said as he left to go get me coffee. I sat there at the table staring off into nowhere...

"How in the hell did I get here?" I asked out loud.

"Here Beautiee," Attorney Smalls said as he sat down with two cups of coffee... "Did you give them a statement?"

"Keisha and Troy did," I answered.

"Who's Keisha and Troy?"

"My neighbors... and my friends... I answered as I teared up...

"You're gonna get through this Beautiee... I gotchu..." he said as he came over to me and gave me a hug. "Let me sit here," he said as he pulled the chair up beside me..."

"If it weren't for Keisha and Troy – I'da been alone..." I said as I started to cry...

"Beautiee?"

"Yes?"

"Did they both give a statement to the police?"

"They both talked to Katina," I answered.

"Do you know what they said?"

"No..." I answered as he handed me some tissues...

"Do I need to be concerned about their statements?"

"No."

"Okay – I'll get a copy of them anyway – what happened at the hospital?"

"They swabbed me for blood samples and they took pictures..."

"Uh huh... what else?"

"They wanted to do a rape kit but I refused..."

"Did you tell them you were raped?"

"No."

"Did they ask you if you were raped?"

"Yes."

"What did you tell them?"

"I told them I wasn't raped."

"Okay – just so we're clear – you were not raped?"

"No – I was not raped..."

"Why the fuck did they want to do a rape kit then?"

"I'on know – maybe because I was covered in blood..."

"Hold on... let me look at these pictures... Oh shit! They didn't let you put any clothes on?"

"I didn't have any to put on..."

"Wait – you mean your friends didn't bring you any clothes?"

"There wasn't any time."

"Wait – how the fuck..."

"After Bazil was shot – they took him out on the stretcher – Troy gave me a robe to put on – I ran out the house, pushed Detective Jones out my way – and screamed for Bazil..." I explained as I cried...   "Thank God they heard me screaming or I wouldn't have made it into the ambulance..." I said as I cried on his shoulder..."

"Hmmmmm... you weren't charged with assaulting an officer... I'm surprised... she actually did you a solid..."

"She didn't do shit!" I screamed... "She saw me running to get in the ambulance with Bazil and she tried to stop me – Fuckin' Bitch!"

"Calm down... I know you're upset – but that is something in your favor..." he said as he took notes... "I need to know what happened... from the beginning..."

"Okay..." I sighed... then finished my coffee... "I invited Sonia over to have sex with me so my husband could watch us and then join in..."

"Uh Huh..." he said as he wrote down what I said...

"That's all you have to say?"

"What am I supposed to say?"

"I'on know... I thought you'd be surprised..."

"I'll be surprised later... continue..."

"Okay... so Sonia agreed to come over..."

"Did Sonia know your husband would be there?"

"Yes."

"And she consented?"

"Yes."

"Okay – continue..."

"So Bazil was watching us have sex... then he joined in..."

"Was that consensual?"

"Yes."

"Did he have sex with both of you?"

"No – just me."

"So – to be clear – Bazil never touched Sonia?"

"Bazil never touched Sonia..."

"Okay – continue..."

"I saw the gun..."

"What gun?"

"I yelled for Bazil to look out but it was too late... he shot Bazil..."

"Who shot Bazil?"

"Trevor shot Bazil..." I answered as I cried...

"Okay – continue..."

"I grabbed Sonia and held her down on top of me... Trevor pointed the gun at me – but he hit Sonia instead..." I cried...

"Okay... then what happened?"

"Trevor screamed Sonia's name... and dropped the gun on the floor... and that's when I realized Sonia set us up..." I cried...

"Sonia set you up?"

"She had to! The only ones that new Sonia was invited over were me and Bazil!" I cried...

"How did Trevor get in your house?"

"I'on know!"

"Okay, okay - what happened next?"

"Trevor came over to Sonia... he started holding her... then he told me it was all my fault and she didn't deserve to die... so I picked up the gun before he could... and I shot him..."

"Oh shit!"

"He tried to shoot me first! It was self-defense!"

"I agree with you... but the defense will argue..."

"They'll argue that I should have let him pick up the gun and try again?"

"You have a point..."

"Exactly..."

"So – to be clear – Trevor was not invited to your house?"

"No."

"And – to be clear – you have no idea how Trevor got in your house?"

"No."

"Where was Trevor when he shot Bazil?"

"He was in my bedroom..."

"He was in your bedroom? And he wasn't invited?"

"No – I never, ever, invited Trevor to my house..."

"Okay Beautiee – I need to ask you something..."

"Okay..."

"Do you have any idea why Trevor would want to kill you or Bazil?"

"I know exactly why Trevor wanted us dead..."

"Why?"

"Because... Bazil and Trevor were lovers..."

"Whhhaaaattt!?"

"Bazil and Trevor were lovers – is that going to come out in court?"

"Yes..."

"Oh well..."

"So... if they were lovers... why did he want y'all dead?"

"Because... Bazil told him it was over between them..."

"Wait – Trevor wanted to kill Bazil because Bazil broke up with him... to be with you?"

"Yes..."

"Damn..." he sighed as he continued taking notes... "Is there anything else I need to know?"

"Yes..."

"Okay..."

"Bazil and Trevor have been lovers since they were in prison together..."

"I'm glad you're telling me this – that prosecuting attorney is a real Bitch – she likes to pull surprises – I'm glad we'll be one up on her ass... okay... take a look at this and tell me what you think..." he said as he pushed the pad over to me with a statement...

"I invited Sonia to my house to have sex while my husband watched. The sex was consensual. Sonia and I were having sex and my husband joined in. While we were having sex, I saw the gun and yelled for Bazil to watch out, but he couldn't move fast enough and was shot. Trevor pointed the gun at me to shoot me but because Sonia was on top of me, he shot her instead. Trevor dropped the gun on the floor, ran over to Sonia, told me it was all my fault, and Sonia didn't deserve to die. At that point, I feared for my life so I picked the gun up off the floor and shot Trevor."

"How's that?" he asked as I read it... I couldn't answer him right away... I just burst into tears...

"I'll sign it..."

"Okay – once you sign this – don't answer any questions..."

"Okay..."

"You'll be in here for tonight – but I'll get you out of here first thing tomorrow – can you make bail?"

"I'll put up my house..."

"You can't put up your house... it's in Bazil's name..."

"I said I'll put up 'MY' house..."

"Your house?"

"Yes... in Bridgeport..."

"Okay – hang in there Beautiee..." he said as he hugged me... "You ready?"

"Yea... I'm ready..." I said as I signed the statement...

"We're ready," he said after opening the door...

"Is your client ready to make a statement?" Katina asked as she sat down at the table...

"Here's her statement," he said as he pushed it to her...

"Really?" she said as she started reading it...

"That's her statement."

"This some bullshit!"

"That's up to the prosecutor."

"Whatever..." she said as she stood up... "I just want this day to be over... come with me Beautiee..."

"May I have a moment with my attorney?"

"Sigh..." she breathed as she left the room and stood outside...

"Thank you," I whispered as I gave him a hug..."

"You're welcome," he said as he tried to pull away...

"Get the surveillance..." I whispered in his ear as Katina came back into the room...

"Are you done?"

"Yes..."

"C'mon..." she said as I followed her to the holding cell.

Twisted Beautiee 5

"Good morning..." Bazil breathed in my ear as he kissed me awake...

"What time is it?" I moaned as I turned to face him and stretched...

"It's time for us to plan our honeymoon..." he breathed as he kissed me...

"I can't wait..."

"Neither can I..."

"Let's see... I came in Connecticut..."

"I don't understand..."

"I'm counting the places I've had orgasms..." I laughed...

"Oh... I see..." he laughed...

"I came in Connecticut..."

"That's one..." he breathed as he kissed me...

"I came in Las Vegas..."

"That's two..." he breathed as he kissed me again...

"I came in New Jersey..."

"New Jersey?"

"On the plane... remember?"

"That's three..." he breathed as he kissed me again...

"I'm gonna cum in Nassau..."

"That's four..." he breathed as he kissed me again, this time putting his tongue in my mouth...

"Mmmm... where will I cum next?" I breathed...

"Well..." he breathed as he kissed me again...

"You could cum in here..."

"I could..."

"Let's go downstairs..."

"Okay..."

"I'll make us coffee..."

"Okay..."

"I'll make breakfast..."

"Okay..."

"You let me know where you wanna cum..."

"Okay..."

"And I'll make you cum..."

"Okay!" I squealed as I jumped up out the bed, threw on my robe, and ran downstairs to the kitchen...

"I guess you really wanna cum..." Bazil laughed...

"I do!"

"Okay, okay!" he laughed... "Le'me make coffee..." he said as he took out everything he needed. I sat there watching him intently as he added the water to the pot...

"You're making a big pot of coffee..."

"I am..."

"Hmmm... I guess I'll have to wait and see..."

"It won't be long..." he said as the pot started brewing...

"Hmmm... maybe I wanna cum on your desk again..." I sighed...

"Okay..." Bazil acknowledged as he took two cups out of the cabinet, put them on the counter, and went over to the refrigerator...

"Oh – is it cold outside? Maybe I can cum in the pool!"

"Okay..." Bazil acknowledged as he made our coffee, put the cups on the table, sat in the chair, opened his robe, and smiled at me mischievously...

"Oh my goodness..." I sighed as I got up and went over to him... "You have a serious issue that needs to be addressed..."

"I do..." he agreed as he took a sip of his coffee...

"As much as I'd love to sit on your dick right now... I'm afraid that won't be enough..."

"You could start by sitting on my dick..." Bazil said as he pulled me closer...

"Wait here – I'll be right back..." I said as I hurried out of the kitchen. When I came back, I had a pillow from the sofa in the library...

"Beautiee... what..."

"Drink your coffee Bazil..." I commanded as I picked up my coffee, took a few sips, dropped the pillow on the floor, got down on my knees in front of him, and took his dick in my mouth...

"Beautiee..." he moaned. I took my time taking his dick in my mouth all the way down his shaft so he could feel the warmth...

"Mmmm hmmmm..." I hummed on his dick and then I took it out my mouth...

"Damn..."

"Drink some more coffee..." I commanded as I picked up my cup, drank some more, and put it back down on the table. I waited for Bazil to drink some more coffee and put his cup down and then I took his dick in my mouth again...

"Beautiee... Shit..." he breathed as he held my head and started fucking my mouth...

"Uh uh..." I said before I took his dick out my mouth again...

"Beautiee..."

"Finish your coffee..." I commanded as I picked up my cup, finished my coffee, and put the cup down on the table. I watched as Bazil picked up his cup and swallowed the rest of his coffee so fast that he spilled some out his mouth...

"Aww... you spilled some..." I sighed and then I took his dick in my mouth again...

"Fuck!" he breathed as he grabbed my head and fucked my mouth... "That's it... Suck it..." he growled as I relaxed my throat and he hit my tonsils... "I'm Cummmmiiinnngggg..... Uuuuugggghhhh!" I swallowed and continued sucking as Bazil played in my hair... "Beautiee..." he whispered. I took his dick out my mouth and looked up at him...

'Yes my Thirst Quencher?"

"Come here..." he said as he helped me up off my knees. Bazil picked up the pillow; I picked up our cups, and took them over to the counter...

"Beautiee... what are you doing?"

"I'm getting us some more coffee..." I said as I smiled at him mischievously. Bazil watched as I made us coffee and brought it back to the table...

"I think that's my new favorite way to have coffee..." he breathed...

"I'm glad you enjoyed it..."

"Have you decided how you want to cum?"

"Not yet..."

"Maybe you should cum the way I did..." he said as he put the pillow on the floor in front of me and dropped down on his knees... "Finish your coffee..." he commanded. I picked up my coffee and gulped it down as quick as I could, stopping twice because it was hot... "Spread your legs..." he commanded as he deliberately took his time finishing his coffee... "Come here..." he breathed as he pulled me down in the chair, put my legs on his shoulders, and dove in...

"Baaazzziiilll!" I moaned as I grabbed his head and started riding his face...

"Yes Beautiee... that's it..."

"Huh... Huh... Huh..." Bazil started thrusting his tongue inside my pussy and put his nose underneath the hood of my clit...

"Bazil... Haaa... Haaa.... Haaa...." Bazil took his tongue out my pussy, put two fingers in my pussy, and began massaging my G-spot as he continued licking, sucking, and slurping... and my legs trembled.... "Bazil... Haaa... Haaa.... Yes... Yes... Yes... Don't stop... I'm cummmiinnng... I'm cummmiinnng... I'm CUMMMIINNNG! AAAGGGGGHHH!" Bazil took his fingers out my pussy but continued licking and sucking softly as I clamped my legs around his head...

"Wow..."

"Wow is right..." I breathed...

"You want more..."

"Yesss..."

"I need to eat first..." he said as he took my legs down off his shoulders, stood up, and helped me up...

"You just ate..." I breathed as he pulled me into a kiss...

"I certainly did..." he breathed.

Twisted Starr

"Hey Thompson – look at that pretty lil' thing right there..." Chandler said, pointing in my direction...

"She sure is pretty..." Officer Thompson agreed...

"To bad she 'about to be arrested..." Chandler sighed...

"For what? Being pretty isn't a crime..."

"Being pretty isn't a crime... but prostitution is..."

"Oh shit! Really?"

"Only one way to find out..." Chandler said as he got up, came outside and walked towards me. "Hello..." he said.

"Hi..." I responded coolly...

"You have nice eyes..."

"Thank you..."

"Can I buy you a cup of coffee?" he asked, hoping he could lure me into the diner...

"Sigh... sure... why not... looks like I missed my bus again..." I said as I turned towards him and looked at him.

"What time is the next bus?"

"Not for another hour."

"Come sit with me - I'll buy you dinner to go with your coffee…"

"That sounds nice – thank you…" I said as I walked towards him with a smile…

"Gotcha!" he thought to himself as I walked past him into the diner and sat at a table near the door….

"Shit – I'ma enjoy dinner, I'ma enjoy coffee, and I'ma be out!" I thought to myself as he came over to the table and sat down…

"What's your name?" he asked as he sat down…"

"Waitress – could you bring us some menus – and some coffee?" I asked, ignoring his question…

"Can I get your name… please?"

"Sure officer – as soon as I get yours…" I smiled.

"Here's your menus…" the waitress said as she came over to the table with the menus and a pot of coffee… "I'll be right back…" she said as she went to get two cups…

"Damn - was I that obvious?" he asked…

"Hell yea!" I laughed…

"Well…" he said as he leaned over and took my hand… "Thank you for allowing me to buy you dinner…" he said as he picked up my hand and kissed it…

"Ooohhh… an officer… and a gentleman… you get brownie points for that…" I blushed…

"Here's your coffee…" the waitress said as she placed the cups on the table and poured us coffee…

"May I?" he asked as he picked up the spoon and began pouring sugar into my coffee…

"Yes please…" I said as I made eye contact with him…

"How many would you like?" he asked, smiling mischievously…

"As many as you'd like to give me..." I answered, smiling mischievously. He over-poured three spoons of sugar into my coffee, opened three creamers, added them to my coffee, stirred it, then watched as I picked up the cup and started drinking it...

"Mmmm.... Perfect..." I breathed...

"Glad you like it..." he smiled as he over-poured three spoons of sugar into his coffee, opened thee creamers, added them to his coffee, stirred it, picked it up, and started drinking...

"Lose your partner..." I said. He spit his coffee back into his cup he laughed so hard...

"Yo Thompson – I'ma holla at you later..." he yelled across to Thompson...

"Aiight – Sarge – later..." Thompson said as he left the diner.

"Oooohhh... Sarge? As in Sergeant?" I asked...

"Yea..." he answered...

"Are you ready to order?" the waitress asked...

"Yes – I'll have a bacon cheeseburger deluxe – hold the coleslaw..." I said as I finished my coffee...

"I'll have the same..." he said as he finished his coffee...

"More coffee?" the waitress asked...

"No thank you..." I answered...

"None for me either..." he answered. The waitress left to place our orders and we made eye contact again...

"So... Sergeant... I'll tell you my name... if you'll tell me yours..." I said...

"Chandler..."

"Hmmm... Chandler... I like that..." I said as I smiled...

"So... who do I have the pleasure of dinning with this evening?" Chandler asked...

"Starr... my name is Starr..."

"Pleased to meet you Starr..." he said as he leaned forward and kissed me on the cheek...

"Nice meeting you too Chandler..." I blushed...

"You live around here?"

"I live about an hour away from here..."

"It takes you an hour to get home from here?"

"Yea..."

"So... are you just getting off work?"

"Kinda..."

"Kinda?"

"Yea..."

"So... where do you 'kinda' work?" he asked, emphasizing the word 'kinda' with his fingers...

"I don't really wanna talk about that..." I said putting my head down..."

"Sorry... we can talk about something else... if you want..." he said as he took my hand...

"I'm actually looking for a job..."

"Oh... Okay..."

"I'm on unemployment – but it's about to run out – I need to find something before it does..." I said...

"Well... you already know I'm a Sergeant..."

"Yes I know..." I said as I smiled...

"Have you ever thought about civil service?"

"Yea..."

"You ever take a civil service exam?"

"No..."

"You should – the pay is good – and so are the benefits..."

"I'm not sure I'm qualified..."

"As long as you don't have any felonies you're qualified..."

"Really?" I asked as the waitress came with our food and put it on the table...

"Oh yea – all you need is a high school or equivalency diploma for an entry level position – but you're getting unemployment so I know you have experience..." Chandler said as he picked up his burger and bit into it...

"Damn!" I laughed..."I thought I was hungry!"

"You ain't the only one – these burgers are slammin'!" he said as he took another bite...

"Oh damn – my bus just left – shit!"

"I'll make sure you get home..." Chandler said as he put his hand on mine...

"Okay... thank you..." I said as I picked up my burger and took a bite... "Oh my God!" I moaned...

"Told you!" Chandler laughed...

"So tell me about you..." I said as I continued eating...

"What would you like to know?"

"Well..." I said in between bites... "Are you single?"

"Are you interested?"

"Not really..." I answered as I started eating my fries.   Chandler sat there quiet.   "I was just playing Chandler – I'm sorry..." I said as I took his hand...

"Really?" Chandler asked...

"Really..." I answered...

"Yes... I'm single..."

"So am I... but I have a feeling that's about to change..." I smiled...

"Is that right?" Chandler asked as he finished his fries...

"Yea..." I smiled.   Chandler smiled back at me making eye contact.

"Shall we get dessert?"

"Naaa... I always get disappointed when I order dessert from dinners..."

"Trust me..." Chandler said as he took my hand..."

"Okay..."

"Waitress?" Chandler called out...

"I'll be right there honey..." she answered as she finished taking an order at another table. We kept looking into each other's eyes without speaking until the waitress came over to the table...

"What can I getcha?" she asked...

"Two apple pie alamode..." Chandler answered...

"Ooohhh... that sounds good..." I breathed. Chandler and I took each other's hands and looked into each other's eyes as the waitress walked away to get our dessert. We didn't speak to each other but we rubbed each other's hands on the table. I knew this wasn't a good idea but when your body's been deprived, it seeks what it craves, his touch felt good, and I was starving...

"Here ya go..." the waitress said as she placed the apple pie and ice cream on the table...

"Thank you..." Chandler said as the waitress walked away...

"Mmmm..." I said as I tasted it... "You're right... this is good..."

"Told you..." he laughed as he started eating...

"You like that..."

"Like what?"

"Saying I told you so..." I laughed as I licked my spoon...

"Yea... I do..." he laughed as he took another spoonful of apple pie and ice-cream. I finished my plate, put my hands up under my chin, placed my elbows on the table, and watched Chandler finish his dessert. Chandler finished his dessert, took my hands from under my chin, and held them in his until the waitress brought the check to the table... "I guess I'll get you home now..." he said as he stood up from the table...

"I guess you will..." I said as I stood up. We both walked to the register, Chandler paid the check, and then we left the diner. "My car's right around the corner..." he said as he put his arm around me. I put my arm around him and we walked to his car. When we got to his car, he opened the door, waited for me to get in, and then closed the door. I reached over to the other side to unlock the door before he could open it...

"Thanks – but I have the key..." he laughed as he sat down and closed the door...

"I know..." I laughed. Chandler started the car, and then turned to look at me...

"Where to?"

"See that bus at the light?"

"Yea..."

"Follow that bus..."

"Follow the bus?"

"Yea – follow that bus..."

"It'll take me longer to get you home that way..." he laughed...

"I know..." I said as I took his hand. Chandler smiled, put the car in drive, and followed the bus. Every time the bus stopped, Chandler stopped, and each time he stopped, he looked over at me, smiling. This went on for about 45 minutes and then I spoke... "Stop here..."

"Okay..." Chandler said as he slowed down to a stop...

"Make a right..."

"Okay..."

"Make this next right..."

"Okay..."

"We're here..." I said as I let go of Chandler's hand and unbuckled the seat belt. I watched Chandler unbuckle his seat belt and I waited for him to open his door and get out the car. He closed the door, walked around to the front of the car to the passenger side and opened the door for me... "Thank you..." I said as I got out the car. When I stood up, Chandler closed the door and pulled me into a kiss before I could object, but I didn't object – I kissed him back as he pinned me against the car...

"Can I see you again?" he breathed...

"Yes... I'd like that..." I breathed as I moved out from underneath him...

"Can I come in?"

"Good night Chandler..." I laughed as I went upstairs. Chandler stood there watching me as I opened the door, went inside, and closed it. After I closed the door, I opened the window and stuck my head out... "You're still here!" I yelled...

"I never got your number!" he yelled...

"I know where you work! I'll call you!"

"Okay! Good night!" I watched Chandler get into his car and drive off, and then I closed my window. I started to go towards the kitchen but my phone rang, so I stopped to answer it...

"You have a collect call from an inmate at the Bridgeport Correctional Facility – will you accept the call?"

"Yes I will..." I said...

"Hey Starr..."

"Hey Mommy..."

"How'd everything go?"

"Oh Mommy... it was wonderful..." I sighed...

"Starr... please don't tell me... you fucked him – didn't you?"

"Not yet... but I'm going to..."

"Starr! What the hell's a matter with you?"

"Nothing!"

"Starr – I need you to stay focused!"

"Oh I'm focused alright..." I laughed...

"Dammit Starr! I didn't set this up for you to get some dick – I set this up so we could get revenge!"

"Well – I'ma get some dick whether you set it up or not..." I laughed...

"Starr... baby... please listen to your mother..."

"Mommy – you don't have to worry about me – I'm taking care of myself..."

"You're barely taking care of yourself – you don't have a job – please girl – you're all I have..." she said as she started crying...

"Please don't cry Mommy – I promise – I'm okay..." I said as tears formed in my eyes...

"You promise?"

"Yes Mommy – I promise..."

"Okay then – tell me about your date..."

"It went just like you said it would..."

"He saw you at the bus stop?"

"Yep."

"I knew it! Did he offer to buy you coffee?"

"Yep."

"That's his M.O. – he knows you're not a trick now..."

"Ma!"

"Starr – that's how they trap tricks – Officer Thompson sits in the diner, Sergeant Chandler offers to buy coffee, the trick offers pussy for money – next thing you know – bam!"

"Ma... are you saying he played me tonight?"

"No baby – I'm not saying that at all – if he wasn't interested in you he wouldn't have invited you into the diner..."

"Mommy?"

"Yea?"

"How'd you know he invited me into the diner?"

"You said your night was wonderful..."

"Yes... I did..."

"Mary – time's up!" I heard the Warden yell...

"Five more minutes... please..." my mother pleaded...

"Okay Mary – but don't make it obvious I gave you extra time – I'm gonna come back and act like you snuck extra time..."

"Okay – thanks..." my mom whispered...

"Tell me about your date Starr..."

"Mommy – we held hands, we ate, we laughed, and we kissed..."

"I love it when you're happy – but be careful baby..."

"I Will Mommy – he's gonna help me get a job..."

"No! You can't do that!"

"Why Mommy?"

"They fingerprint you and run a background check on you for civil service jobs..."

"Chandler says as long as I don't have any felonies I can get a job Mommy..."

"Starr – listen to me – they'll take your fingerprints – they'll do a background check – and they'll find out you're my daughter..."

"Oh shit – that's right – okay Mommy – I'll find another way..."

'Mary! Didn't I tell you time's up? Get off that phone – now!"

"I love you Starr!" my mom said as the call was disconnected...

"I love you too Mommy..." I whispered out loud as I hung up the phone...

Twisted Starr 3

"Hey Keisha..."

"Girl – what's wrong?"

"Nothing..."

"Oh so you just knocked on my door for nothing?"

"If you're not up for company I'll just come back another time..."

"Git yo' ass in here..." Keisha said as she grabbed Beautiee into a hug... and Beautiee started crying...

"Is Troy here?"

"No..."

"Good..." Beautiee said as she went into the kitchen and started making coffee. Keisha watched her intently without speaking. Beautiee made coffee, got the cups, creamer, sugar, and put everything on the table, and then sat down...

"Bazil..." Keisha said as they made their coffee and started drinking...

"I wish I wasn't pregnant..."

"Oh damn – what the fuck happened?"

"Oh no – I'm just saying I wish I wasn't pregnant because I want a drink..." Beautiee laughed...

"Oh thank God – ya'll be scaring the shit outta me!" Keisha laughed...

"I'm sorry..."

"You ain't gotta be sorry – life happens..."

"Damn sure does..."

"So... you wanna tell me what you were crying about?"

"How much coffee you have left?"

"I have espresso if you need something stronger..."

"Oh hell yea!"

"Okay – we'll finish this and then I'll make some espresso..."

"Okay..."

"Beautiee..." Keisha said as she took her hand... "This isn't good for you... or the baby..."

"I know..."

"What's going on?"

"A lot..." Keisha got up from the table and put on the espresso maker and started the pot...

"I can listen while I'm making coffee..."

"Starr has a job..."

"That's good..."

"She works at the University in New Haven..."

"Okay..."

"She works Monday through Thursday - 8:30 – 4:30 - Friday 8:30 to 1:30 – Saturday 9 to 1..."

"She likes the job?"

"She loves it..."

"That's good..."

"She's really sweet..."

"That's nice..."

"I wish she was my daughter..."

"Aww..."

"They came to see us on Tuesday..."

"Starr and Chandler..."

"They good?"

"They went to City Hall..."

"They got their marriage license?"

"Yea..."

"They set a date?"

"Yea..."

"When they getting' married?"

"June 6th..."

"Damn – when did you plan on sending invitations?"

"I'm not..."

"So we're not invited?"

"You stupid..." Beautiee laughed...

"Okay – I'ma put this on my calendar..."

"It's in Boston at the Taylor Bed & Breakfast – they plan everything – you just show up..."

"Oh that's nice – they book it yet?"

"I took care of their wedding and their honeymoon on Tuesday..."

"Damn – I wish I knew you when we got married..." Keisha laughed...

"I love Starr – she's so in love – she's so happy – I just wanted to do that for her..."

"You did that for Bazil too..."

"Yea..."

"Here..." Keisha said as she put the espresso on the table...

"Keisha – you want me to drink this straight up?"

"Drink!"

"Okay, okay!" Beautiee laughed as she drank it... "Uggh!"

"You gonna talk now or do I have to make you drink another shot?"

"Fuck it – hit me again – but this time you're drinking with me..."

"Aiight – bet!" Keisha said as they both took a shot of espresso...

"Uugh!" they both said in unison...

"Starr got an eviction notice..."

"Oh shit!"

"Her mother was supposed to be out by Friday or Starr was gonna get evicted and lose her Section 8..."

"Her mother had to go to the shelter?"

"She was..."

"What happened?"

"The realtor called – Starr got her keys to her new place on Thursday..."

"Starr got an apartment?"

"Bazil bought her a co-op in Downtown Bridgeport..."

"Oh wow – he know her mother's staying there?"

"Yea..."

"And he's okay with that?"

"He wasn't... but I talked to him..."

"Oh so you fucked him and he gave in..." Keisha laughed..."

"No Keisha – I talked to him..."

"You did?"

"Yea – I just told him as long as Starr was worried about her mother she wouldn't be alright – she just got a job, she's getting married – she wouldn't be right if her mother was in the shelter..."

"You treat Starr like she's your daughter..."

"She is... Bazil said her mother could stay there if she signed a lease and agreed to pay rent – and the Triflin

Bitch called Bazil and told him she wasn't signing shit and she wasn't payin' shit!"

"So wait – she expects Bazil to take care of her too?"

"Exactly..."

"Where the fuck they do that at?"

"Girl I'on know – gime another shot!" Beautiee laughed as they both took another shot...

"Uugh! How this shit worse than liquor?" Keisha laughed...

"I know – right?" Beautiee laughed...

"So what's Starr gonna do?"

"Starr told us her mother was gonna have to go to the shelter if she didn't wanna sign the lease and pay rent – and girl – get this – they had a fight!"

"What?! She hit Starr?"

"Starr said she called Bazil a Ratchet Bastard and Chandler heard them fighting when he came to get her – and girl – you ain't heard the best part..."

"Tell me..."

"She called Starr a Lil' Bitch!"

"What?! Oh she good – I would'a told my mother get the fuck out my house – she good anyway – she'da moved in with y'all until she got married..."

"Right! But Starr was cryin' to me talkin' about how much she loves her mother and it hurt her feelings..."

"Aww..."

"I told her her mother didn't mean it..."

"Yes she did – she meant that shit!"

"Maybe she did – but I told Starr she's mad at her father..."

"You good..."

"I love her..."

"Bazil's a lucky man..."

"Sometimes he takes that for granted..."

"I knew it – what the fuck did he do?"

"I'm gettin' to it..."

"Okay..."

"So... on Wednesday... Chandler had lunch with Bazil and Mary..."

"Oh boy..."

"My husband thought the shit was funny..."

"What happened?"

"Chandler told them both he was tired of Starr being in the middle of their shit!"

"No he didn't!"

"Yes girl – here's the funny part though..." I laughed...

"Tell me – I wanna laugh too..."

"Chandler told them if they kept putting Starr in the middle of their shit he would make sure they didn't see Starr again!"

"Aaaahaaaa! Aaaahaaaa!" they both laughed...

"Wait – Chandler thinks he can stop Bazil – hell – nobody stops Bazil!" she laughed...

"Girl – I ain't done..."

"Oh hell – my stomach..."

"Bazil told him he couldn't stop him from seeing his daughter..." Beautiee laughed... "and Chandler said try me!"

"Aaaahaaaa! Aaaahaaaa!" they both laughed...

"You lyin!"

"No girl!"

"Go 'head Chandler!"

"I know – right?"

"This is good – but you still ain't tell me what Bazil did..."

"I'm getting' to it!"

"Okay – go 'head..."

"So... Chandler pulled out a lease..."

"No!"

"Yes girl – and he told Mary Bazil made you an offer – and you're gonna take it!"

"I fuckin' love Chandler!"

"Me too girl!"

"What'd she say?"

"She tried it – but Chandler told her Starr doesn't need her Section 8 anymore – the rent is only paid until the end of May – so she doesn't have a choice – unless she wants to go to the shelter – but don't expect Starr to come visit!"

"Oh shit!" Keisha said as they high-fived... "Bazil put him up to that?"

"No girl – it was all Chandler..."

"I love it, I love it, I love it! Did she sign it?"

"She signed it..."

"Yeesss!"

"So everybody's happy – Bazil comes home..." Beautiee said as she started crying...

"What happened?"

"He called me to the kitchen... he has fruit, meat, cheese, sparkling cider, balloons, roses..."

"Aww..."

"He tells me he did that for me because of everything I did for his daughter... he tells me how much he loves me... I was so happy..."

"Okay – I'm confused – if you were so happy..."

"I'm getting to that..."

"Oh my God – I can't take it..."

"So... that was Tuesday and Wednesday... now we get to Thursday..."

"Okay..."

"Sheddi calls..."

"Okay – wait – who's Sheddi?"

"The real estate agent..."

"Okay..."

"So she says they can close Friday morning..."

"Okay..."

"So we're celebrating..."

"Yall fuckin'..." Keisha laughed...

"Yea..." Beautiee said as she took out her phone and showed Keisha the picture of Bazil kissing her stomach in the shower...

"Oh wow... that's dope..."

"That was Friday morning..." Beautiee said as she started tearing up. Keisha took Beautiee's hand and Beautiee kept talking... "So they went to the closing... they got the keys... and Bazil came home... I heard him come in... I called him... he didn't answer me... so I went in the kitchen... I threw my arms around his neck... I kissed him... and..." Keisha started rubbing Beautiee's arm as she cried... "He pushed me away from him... and... told... me... to... leave... him... alone..." Keisha got up from the table, went to the bathroom, got a box of tissues... and came back into the kitchen...

"Damn – I know that hurt your feelings – that shit hurt my feelings..." she said as she wiped her eyes along with Beautiee...

"I went in the library and I turned on the computer to do some writing... and Starr called me..."

"What'd she say?"

"She asked me what was wrong – and I told her nothing..."

"She knew you was lyin'..."

"She asked me why I was acting so funny – first her father, then her mother, now me..."

"Something happened at that closing..."

"Starr said her father started acting funny after he had an argument with Smalls..."

"Oh shit..."

"So I went in the kitchen to talk to Bazil... he wasn't there but he left his jacket in the kitchen... and I picked it up... and this letter fell out..." Beautiee said as she started crying again..." That Triflin' Bitch is suing Bazil for back child support..." Beautiee cried...

"So... Smalls served Bazil... at the closing?"

"Yea..." Beautiee sniffed...

"And Bazil comes home... and pushes you away..."

"Yea..."

"See – that's that bullshit!"

"Exactly..."

"He needs to apologize..."

"He apologized yesterday... but I pushed him away from me..."

"You did? Why?"

"I pushed him away because I'm tired..."

"You're tired? Oh shit..."

"I told him you're sorry – and I'm tired..."

"Did he try to explain?"

"I told him I didn't want to hear it..."

"Oh damn – that's not like you..."

"I'm tired Keisha – I asked him how many fuckin' times do we have to go through shit before he fuckin' gets it?"

"You right..."

"He pushed me away... after everything we've been through... after everything I've done... and that hurt..."

"Damn Beautiee... I'm sorry..."

"It took everything in me not to choke that Triflin' Bitch yesterday..."

"Wait – what?"

"I promised Starr we would go shopping for wedding dresses... and I promised her I'd pick up her mother..."

"Oh hell no – you good..."

"What was I supposed to do Keisha?"

"And Bazil pushed you away from him... and you cryin' – that mutha fucka should be cryin'..."

"He was..."

"Good..."

"I love him so much... but I'm tired... he hurts me – he's sorry – then he hurts me again... and I'm tired..."

"You're pregnant too..."

"I know..."

"You're emotional..."

"I've always been emotional..."

"So whatchu gonna do?"

"I slept in the guest room last night... and I locked the door so Bazil couldn't get in..."

"Oh shit! You that mad?"

"Keisha?"

"Yea?"

"I had to lock the door..."

"Why?"

"It was the only way I could stop myself from jumpin' on his dick..."

"Oh so you not mad..."

"It really hurt my feelings... and I'm really tired..."

"You not gonna talk about it?"

"I just wanna see Starr and Chandler get married... she was so happy yesterday trying on dresses..."

"I bet her mother was too..."

"Yea..."

"She didn't say anything to you?"

"She tried – and I shut her down..."

"You did?"

"I told her don't open her fuckin' mouth about my husband – and don't tell me how sorry you are – show me – fix it!"

"Girl – I'on know if I could do it – you good..."

"If it wasn't for Starr..."

"You really love her..."

"I do... she's actually worried about me... she told me she knew something was going on with me and her father and it made her sad..."

"Aww..."

"I can't ruin her wedding Keisha..."

"So you not gonna tell her?"

"No..."

"What about Bazil? Ya'll need to talk..."

"Girl... I don't need to talk..." I laughed...

"Oh Lord – I can't - y'all make me sick..." she laughed... "but for real though – he didn't mean to hurt your feelings..."

"Keisha?"

"What?"

"Did you just defend Bazil?"

"I know – right?" she laughed...

"I'll talk to him..."

"Good..."

Beautiee went back in the house, she went straight upstairs to the guest room... and bust out laughing. While she was at Keisha & Troy's house, Bazil took the door off the guest room to keep her from locking him out and, to be honest, it made her smile. She shook her head, sat down on the bed, and saw an envelope addressed to her, so she picked it up, took out his letter and started reading...

Dear Beautiee,

I'm sorry. I know you're tired – tired of me hurting you - tired of me being sorry for hurting you – and tired of me hurting you – please believe me – I swear I don't mean to – I just can't help it. I know that's no excuse – but I'm being honest – and I'm trying. All you wanted to do was love me and I should've let you – but I was in so much pain I couldn't let you love me. When I pushed you away from me I was being selfish – but I can't help that either – I was too deep in my feelings at the moment to realize how hurt you were – I know that's no excuse – but I need you to understand it had nothing to do with you and everything to do with me. I've never had a woman come and comfort me – especially after I pushed them away – the way you did. It's easy when I'm loving you and comforting you because I'm the man – I'm supposed to do that – but it's hard for me to be vulnerable – especially in difficult moments. When I pushed you away it wasn't because I didn't want you – I'll always want you – it was because I was angry that Mary got to me – again – I was angry at myself for letting her get to me – and I was angry at myself for being weak – and instead of telling you how I was feeling I pushed you away. Starr was so happy at the closing and I had to sit there and pretend that I was happy when the truth is – I wanted to choke the shit out of Conrad for taking the case – and I also wanted to choke the shit outta my friend – my brother – Smalls – for serving me that fuckin' paper.

Now that you know how I feel – please forgive me. I can't promise you I won't hurt you again – but I can promise you I'm gonna let you love me – because I need you to.

Love,

Bazil

Beautiee sat there and cried. She was so happy Bazil shared what he was going through and what he was feeling, she took out the same pad and pen he used to write her that letter and she wrote one back...

Dear Bazil,

Thank you. I'm crying as I'm writing this – not because I'm hurt – but because I'm happy. I'm happy that you let me know what you were going through and how you were feeling – and I'm sorry you were hurting. I know it's hard for you to be vulnerable but as you said – you're a man – and just like the rest of us – you have a heart – and feelings – and you can be hurt too. I'm also sorry you've never known comfort from another woman – but I'm happy to know that I'm able to comfort you when you need it most – and I will comfort you whenever you need me to. When I read that letter I was hurt for all of us – and I was hurt for your friend – your brother – Smalls – because I know it broke his heart to have to serve you that paper. You said in your letter you wanted to choke the shit outta Conrad – well – I wanna choke the shit outta Mary. It was all I could do to keep my composure yesterday when we picked Mary up to go shopping for wedding dresses – and I had to check her too – she brought your name up and I told her don't open your fuckin' mouth about my husband – and don't tell me how sorry you are – show me – fix it!

I swear if Starr wasn't getting married – but she is – and I love her – and I love you – but when this wedding is over –

we're going into battle – and we're going to take that Triflin
Bitch down together.

Love,

Beautiee

Beautiee took her letter, put it in an envelope, went into
the bedroom, handed it to Bazil, and sat down on the bed
beside him as he read it. He started crying and she cried
too. He took her face in his hands and kissed her and when
he did, they couldn't keep their hands off each other...

"Bazil..."
"Beautiee...
"Bazil..."
"Beautiee...
"Hmmm...."
"Ugghhh...
"Hmmm..."
"Ugghh..."
"Yeess..."
"Fuck... shit... shit..."
"Oh God..." Beautiee and Bazil held on to each other
for dear life and fucked for the next hour...
"Ooohhh...."
"Ummppphhh..."
"Ooohhh...
"Mmmppphhh..." It was a battle between the sexes
as Bazil and Beautiee took turns flipping each other
around on the bed and when Bazil put Beautiee's legs up
on his shoulders and started fuckin' her hard and deep...
she lost it...
"Oh God... Bazil! I'm cumming!"

"Uugghhh! Uuugghhh! Uugghh!" Bazil held Beautiee in position for a few moments before he put her legs down and lay down beside her...

"Bazil..." she breathed...

"Yes... Beautiee..." he breathed as he kissed her...

"That... was... so... fuckin... good..."

"I know..." he said as he smiled mischievously...

"Fuck you..." she laughed...

"You just did..."

"I love you..."

"I love you too..."

"You ready for battle?"

"With you by my side? Hell yea!" Bazil said as he pulled Beautiee into a kiss and they continued kissing and holding each other.

Twisted Mary

"Uh uh – le'me stop you right there!" Chandler snapped... "This here – we're not doing this – this not what we came her for..."

"I understand that Chandler – but Beautiee needs to understand that she's not the grandmother – I am – and my grandchild will not be calling her son Jay..."

"Mommy! Stop it!"

"Really Mary?" Beautiee asked... "You can't let them have their moment?"

"Mary – I'ma need you to understand something quick – this is our child – not yours – not theirs – and my child will call his uncle Jay, Jay – 'cause that's his name – until his parent's change it – understand?"

"Not if I'm around he won't..."

"Starr – I know that's your mother – but if this how she's gonna act – then she doesn't have to be around..."

"Chandler – you can't stop me from seeing my grandchild..."

"Mommy!" Starr said as she started crying...

"Mary – what is wrong with you? Why would you do that to her?" Beautiee asked as she got up to hug Starr...

"Oh my – you're concern is so convenient..." I said...

"Chandler – please – can you get the waitress? I need coffee for this..." Beautiee laughed...

"May I take your orders?" the waitress asked as she came over with a pot of coffee and 5 mugs...

"Yes – we'll start with this pot of coffee – I'm gonna need more than one cup..." Beautiee said as she took the pot and poured everyone a cup...

"None for me thank you..." I said. Beautiee ignored me and poured it anyway... "I said none for me!" I snapped...

"Its fine – I'll drink it – damn!" Beautiee said...

"Can we order some food – please?" Bazil laughed...

"Sure..." Chandler answered... "Honey – no offense – just bring us some of everything on the breakfast menu..."

"Everything?" the waitress asked...

"Everything... Chandler answered...

"Okay sir – coming right up..." she said as she walked away to place our order...

"Chandler – thank you for breakfast – Mary – just what the fuck is your problem?" Beautiee asked...

"You're acting all concerned and fake – you weren't being so nice when you put Starr out the other day..." I answered...

"See – this the shit I'm talkin' about – Mary – we didn't come here for this!" Chandler snapped...

"Naa... let a Bitch talk Chandler..." Beautiee laughed as she finished her coffee. Bazil sat there drinking his coffee and shaking his head. Chandler threw up his hands...

"For starters – don't call me a Bitch – Bitch!"

"Okay…" Beautiee laughed… "What else you got?"

"I don't like you cursing at my daughter!"

"Starr…" Beautiee said as she turned to her… "Fuck and Ass are very much a part of my vocabulary – if I offended you in any way when I spoke to you – I'm sorry…"

"That's okay Beautiee…"

"Personally I thought you'd be more upset at your mother calling you a Lil' Bitch – but since I'm just your father's baby momma – I guess that ain't none of my business…"

"I'm sorry Beautiee – I shouldn't've said that to you – Chandler told me I was wrong…"

"Thank you Chandler for defending me – but Starr is right – I'm just her father's baby momma – I'm not her mother – my mistake was treating you like you were my daughter – I won't make that mistake again…"

"Beautiee – please don't say that – I love you…"

"I love you too Starr – that won't change…"

"Oh please – you can miss me with the cumbia bullshit – when you were in labor I helped your ass deliver your son – now you wanna act like you don't know who the fuck I am!" I snapped…

"Yes Mary – you certainly did help me – here's a gift certificate to the Classic Nails and Day Spa at Trumbull Mall to repay you for your kindness…" Beautiee said as she handed me an envelope… "Are we done now – or is there something else we need to discuss?"

"Well – now that you mention it – why were you so adamant that I couldn't be invited to your baby shower?"

"I'm so glad you asked me that…" Beautiee said as she picked up a corn muffin, buttered it, and started eating it… "Our friends are throwing us a baby shower to celebrate the birth of our son – they're not throwing us a celebration of baby mommas – personally – I'd rather not

153

have a shower to celebrate the fact that we both have a child with my husband – what would we be doing anyway – taking a trip down memory lane – comparing notes as to who sucked my husband's dick the longest?"

"Beautiee!" Chandler yelled...

"What?" Beautiee asked as the people at the next table looked on...

"Starr's sitting here!"

"Oh please – if she ain't suckin' dick already – she's Bazil's daughter – she will be – are we done now Mary or is there something else you need to address?"

"Actually – there is something else..." I said...

"What is it Mary?"

"Jermoll told me what he did to you – I'm so sorry that happened..." Chandler looked at Bazil and got the answer to his question without even asking as the waitress brought the food to the table...

"Bazil – I can't do this anymore..." Beautiee said as she got up from the table and ran out the restaurant.

Twisted Mary 3

"Mary,

I went to check us out of the hotel. You were sleeping so peacefully I didn't want to disturb you. I'll be back later.

Love,

Wayne"

After he left the note on the table he slipped out the door, closed it quietly, and went to get in the car. He drove to the hotel in silence, parked the car, went into the hotel, and headed for the lounge...

"I might as well get myself some coffee..." he thought to himself as he made the coffee and went upstairs to the room. When he got in the room and closed the door, he couldn't hold it in anymore – he fell to the floor on his knees and sobbed...

"God... please... help me..."

"Yes Wayne..."

"I fucked up..."

"No you didn't..."

"I hurt her so bad... I didn't mean to..."

"I know..."

"It's not fair! Why couldn't that be my child?' Why me? Haven't I suffered enough?"

"It is your child... and... as far as your suffering... that's your choice..."

"I don't understand..."

"You've always wanted children... I've given you another chance... and... instead of realizing how blessed you are... you're suffering..."

"I want to be happy... I love children... but I just can't..."

"You just can't be happy with your wife being pregnant... or... is it that you just can't forgive Bazil?"

"Lord... this isn't about Bazil..."

"Did you forget who you're talking to?" You told your wife you couldn't go through this again... you also told your wife that this was bringing up past hurt... so if it's not about Bazil... who's it about?"

"I never thought of it that way..."

"I know..."

"I love her so much... I just want that baby to be mine..."

"Then why did you tell her to have an abortion?"

"I don't know... I can't deal with it... it broke my heart with Starr..."

"You love Starr... don't you?"

"Yes..."

"You told your wife you forgive her... right?"

"Yes..."

"You're not treating your wife like you forgive her..."

"I know... I'm sorry... I don't know what to do..."

"You know exactly what to do... it's just a matter of what you choose..."

"Lord... I'm not sure I can do this..."

"Wayne... do you trust me?"

"Yes Lord... I trust you..."

"Show me..." Wayne jumped up off the floor, grabbed the suitcases, threw everything in them without bothering to fold the clothes, and hurried out the room.

"Good morning Mr. Robinson – I see you have suitcases – are you finally checking out?" the clerk asked...

"Yes I am..."

"Congratulations... we'll miss you..."

"Thank you..."

"Think you'll be back anytime soon?" she asked as she completed his check out and gave him the paperwork...

"Only God knows..." he answered as he grabbed the paperwork and hurried out the hotel...